DECISIONS
Sybil Norcroft Book Five

Carl Douglass
Neurosurgeon Turned Author Writes with Gripping Realism

Since 1978

PO Box 221974 Anchorage, Alaska 99522-1974
books@publicationconsultants.com—www.publicationconsultants.com

ISBN 978-1-59433-527-3
eISBN 978-1-59433-528-0
Library of Congress Catalog Card Number: 2014960349

Manufactured in the United States of America.

Disclaimer

All of the six novellas in the Sybil Series are works of fiction and should not be construed as representing real persons, places, or events. Some names of real persons and places appear but only for the purpose of creating a setting in the real world or as a mention of historical circumstances. None of the real people or the real places were actually involved in the fictional portrayals found in these short books. All of the events described were created from the author's imagination.

4

Dedication

To my family

Books by Carl Douglass

FICTION

Last Phoenix-A Novel of Betrayal and Revenge, A Story of
the CIA's Phoenix Program

Saga of a Neurosurgeon Series, **Six Books**
  -Young Coyote-**Book One: Garven Wilsonhulme's Way to**
  Success-No Quarter Asked and None Given
  -Anything Goes-**Book Two**
  -Heaven and Hell-**Book Three: Garven Wilsonhulme**
  Takes on All Comers in the Jungle of Modern Competition
  -Long Climb-**Book Four: Young M.D., Garven Wilsonhulme,**
  Engaged in a Social Poker Game of Winner Takes All
  -Academia: The Law of the Jungle-**Book Five: Surgeon**
  in Training, Garven Wilsonhulme, Fang-and-Claw
  Competition for Glory
  -The Vulture and the Phoenix-**Book Six: Neurosurgeon,**
  Garven Wilsonhulme, the Final Great Fight

All in Jest-Renowned Neurosurgeon in the Fight of Her Life

Gog and Magog—Yawm al-Qiyamah, Yawm al-Din, The Day of Judgment

Finders Keepers, Losers Weep-A Novel of Innocence Betrayed and the Search for Restitution

Sheep Dog and The Wolf-A Story of Terrorism and Response, and the Sheep Dogs Who Protect

Trojan Horse in the Belly of the Beast, Three Books
 Though They Come From the Ends of the Earth-Book One
 Dancing with the Devil-Book Two
 Trojan Horse in the Belly of the Beast-Book Three

NOVELLAS

1st Novella-*The End of the Beginning*
2nd Novella-*Uncharted Country, Uncertain Future*
3rd Novella-*Secrets*

4th Novella-*Secrets and Scandals*
5th Novella-*Decisions*
6th Novella-*Running with the Big Dogs*

NONFICTION

On Evolution The Origin of Selection, Order, Progression, and Diversity–out of print

Something About Religion—out of print

Chapter One

It was fitting that the meeting was being held in the world's third tallest building which stretches skyward above the Grand Mosque and the Ka'aba. That fit the soaring ambitions and prejudices of the men in the elaborately decorated room. The room fell silent as the old man entered—a gesture beyond respect and into reverence. Muhammad al Saud ibn Wahhab was generally regarded as the grandest of the grand old men of Islam; and whenever he spoke, it was as if the Prophet, himself—may his name be revered forever—was speaking. Throughout the Kingdom, ibn Wahhab was also a lightning rod of controversy. As a patriarch of the Wahhab family and an intimate of the ruling Saud family, he was considered by many of his countrymen—and more than a few in the government—to have undue influence and power for a man with no official government position. He was widely—but quietly—held to be overly stringent and severe in his views on the practice of Islam in the Kingdom and throughout the world.

His most contentious view was that he was one of the architects of the new Mecca. His Mecca was no longer the humble and strict preserver of Islam's most holy sites in Mecca, Medina, and Mina; he was the leader of a faction within the Wahhab family dedicated to the destruction and removal of such revered sites as *Al Hajar Al Aswad* [the Black Stone] in the Ka'aba which millions of Muslims have kissed for over a thousand years, the *Muqaam Ibrahim* [Place of Abraham] a site inside *Al-Masjid Al-Haram* [the Great Mosque of Mecca built around the Ka'aba], the Zamzam Well, *Jabal Al Rahmah* [The Hill of Forgiveness, Mount Arafat], *Al-Masjid al-Nabawi* [Mosque of the Prophet] in Medina, and of dozens of places of Saudi Arabia's archeological heritage—even cemeteries—where many of the greatest-of-the-great Islamic heroes were laid to rest. He preached against the preservation of Islam's heritage—of Saudi Arabia's heritage—as being unIslamic.

Muhammad al Saud ibn Wahhab and his followers had what was, for them, a valid reason for their objection to all such traditions: in the minds of the Wahhabis, historical sites, and shrines encourage "*shirq*" the unforgivable sin and even capital crimes of idolatry or polytheism. Ibn Wahhab counted among his greatest achievements the construction of the building in which he was standing—the nearly 2,000 foot tall Royal Mecca Clock Tower which soared emblematically over the Grand Mosque and the holy shrine, reducing its historical significance. Over the past decade and a half, ibn Wahhab and the hard-line clerics of his family had worked systematically with the Saudi royal family to transform Mecca and Medina—the two holiest cities in the Islamic world—into a playground, business center for the rich, and the showcase of Saudi Arabian national pride.

The city had become a steel, concrete, and glass megalopolis of high rises, innovative and artistic architectural masterpieces where naked capitalism had trumped the humble dusty destination of the *hajj* [Sacred Pilgrimage]. There are only three sites the Saudis and the Wahhabis have allowed the U.N. to designate World Heritage Sites—and thereby preserve them—none are related to Islam.

The Saudi ruling family agreed with the Wahhabi vision of the Kingdom's and the city's future built from the enormous profits gushing from the seemingly inexhaustible treasure of oil reposing beneath the country's desert sands. Instead of recoiling at the desecration of the places beloved by the humble believers since the advent of Islam, the royal family and their ultra-religious partners—the Wahhab family—reveled in their ability to upstage the decadent West in their own love of capitalism and grandeur. Five-star hotels had long since appeared where affordable rental rooms had served the humble pilgrims coming to the holy cities to celebrate their compliance with the once in a lifetime requirement to participate in the holy pilgrimage—to become a hajji. More moderate Muslims in places like Indonesia, Morocco, the UAE [United Arab Emirates], and even in inordinately strict Shi'ite Iran, were aghast at the audacity of the Wahhabs to trade the sacred for bling.

Muhammad al Saud ibn Wahhab took his place at the dais and began to speak. The quiet murmurs of respectful whispering became reverential silence when he began to talk in his quiet, masterly way.

"Brothers, thank you for your presence here. Many of you have come a long distance to the Holy City. I will be brief.

When I am finished, you will separate into groups as indicated by the numbered cards you all received when you first entered the room. The numbered groups correspond to one or another aspect of the project as I describe it to you. Most of you are already familiar with the overall plan. Today you will begin to learn specifics. Let me once again exhort you to secrecy. It is a dangerous world what with the Great Satan—those *jinns* who serve Shaytan—Little Satan—the sons of Zion, whom our Allah described as the sons of apes and pigs—and those *rafida* among the Tawhid, those *kaffirs* and *Hazaras*, who have rejected the true way and seek to undermine Allah's one way and the Sunnah. Be ever on your guard.

"The Kingdom has nuclear armaments, a fact that appears to be unknown to the decadent West and puts them at peril. Allah has provided us with the means to deliver those weapons. Our purpose today is to devise a detailed set of logistics to deliver the "Wrath of God", as our weapons are known, and to usher in *Yawm al-Qiyamah, Yawm al-Din* [The Day of Judgment]. Be mindful that our mission is sanctioned by our God, and He is with us. He is a just God, and will wreak awful justice out on the Zionist Entity and the land of the heretics. Eventually—with victories there—the rest of the Islamic world will unite to annihilate the Great Satan. Let's get to work, my brothers."

Chapter Two

President's Daily Briefing, Oval Office, The White House, Washington D.C., December 18, 2015, 0800 hrs.
Present: POTUS (NI One), DCIA, DNI, DNSA
Re: Renewed unrest in the Middle-East

"Mr. President," DCIA Martin Edelweiss began his presidential daily briefing, "we have worked for several days on the growing disturbances in a variety of places throughout the Muslim Middle-East. Some patterns are emerging, and our concerns are escalating accordingly. First: Tehran sent a shipload of high explosives to Jizan, a Saudi port town on the Red Sea. An Israeli Naval Intelligence Division Sa'ar 5-class corvette stopped the ship and boarded her in the Arabian Sea just off the coast near the Yemen and Oman border. They found several tons of Russian PVV-5A plastic explosive, Slovakian CHEMEX (C4), TVAREX 4A, man-portable recoilless antitank rocket launcher weapons, rocket propelled grenade launchers, Spanish army M-65s, det-cord, and instantaneous impact fuses for high-explosive shells. The crew obligingly told the Israelis—in return for being able to be put off on Yemeni soil—that their cargo was bound for Jizan and was to be received by al Qaeda operatives. The IDF naval personnel took the Hezbollah militants back to Tel Aviv with them. With a bit of enhanced persuasion, the Hezbollah combatants revealed that al Qaeda intended to attack Saudi government institutions that supported attacks in Iran.

"Second: Iranian defense forces captured what they described as a squad of Saudi Arabian Naval special services NSSU commandos in the coastal city of Bushehr armed with—among other things—German surplus Mk-54 shoulder fired weapons and a truckload of M-388 rounds using an outmoded version of the American Davy Crocket W54 warhead. These weapons are very small and man portable sub-kiloton fission devices; they weigh about 50 pounds and have a yield equivalent to somewhere between 10 or 20 tons of TNT— very close to the minimum practical size and yield for a fission warhead. The Iran newspapers and TV have been full of pictures of the Saudi commandos and their weapons.

"Third: IDF personnel captured a squad of suicide bombers as they were putting on their vests in a seedy Tel Aviv hotel. Mossad told us that there was enough blast power in those suicide vests to level ten square blocks of the capital city. As near as they could determine, the source was Riyadh, not Tehran.

"Fourth: a team of Mossad agents was interdicted in the outskirts of Mashhad, Razavi Khorasan Province. That is Iran's second largest city. The Israeli agents were found when a young shepherd boy saw them hiding in a canal near the city's main electrical power plant. Six of the seven Israelis were killed by IRDF [Iran Refuse Derived Fuels] security forces, and the seventh held out for a week before revealing that he and his mates were from the Mossad. They had enough high explosives and equipment to flatten the power plant.

"This has been the busiest couple of weeks in the area during the last two years. Something's going on over there, Mr. President."

"Yesterday, you gave me some preliminary data on the Saudis getting atomic collaboration from the Pakistanis and the Chinese. Anything new there?" President Willets asked.

"We have an asset in the Saudi *Al Mukhabarat Al A'amah* anti-cyber espionage section, and a very highly placed asset in the Pakistani ISI [Directorate for Inter-Services Intelligence]. Their information is confirmatory: Pakistan sold the Saudis something like 400 pounds of highly enriched uranium six years ago and another 800 the first of this year. We have the truck manifests, shipment numbers, origins, and destinations. That is confirmed. We have some hints that the PRC [Peoples Republic of China] sold the Saudis some—but unknown how much. Secrecy was much better maintained on the part of each side of that transaction or transactions. We really can't confirm that the PRC actually did sell them any. We are still working on it."

"So, what are your conclusions, Director?"

"Saudi Arabia almost certainly does not have a nuclear weapons materials production system. They have been under far too much scrutiny for us or the IAEA [International Atomic Energy Agency] to have missed such production facilities. Iran has half a dozen of them, and their only argument is that their nuclear production is strictly for peaceful purposes. Officially and publicly, the Kingdom is opposed to nuclear weapons within its borders or anywhere else in the Middle-East. The Saudis are signatories of the Nuclear

Non-Proliferation Treaty. The nation is a strong member of the coalition of countries demanding a Nuclear-Weapon-Free Zone in the Middle-East, and is very public and vocal about it. Official U.N. and our intelligence services' studies of nuclear proliferation have not identified Saudi Arabia as a country of concern. They are not on any restrictions lists of the United States."

"I sense a 'but' coming," the president said watching DCIA Edelweiss's face.

"Indeed," Mr. President. "Despite all of the Saudi's protestations and coziness with the U.S., we have a copy of a strategy memo from nearly fifteen years ago which outlined several options for the government to acquire nuclear weapons as deterrents. The paper was adamant about the Kingdom not having aggressive intentions. Since then, several things have happened: 1) The U.S. developed serious concerns about Iran and backed away from assisting the Saudis to purchase enriched uranium for their peaceful uses. This caused a degree of cooling in relations between the Kingdom and the U.S.. 2) That cooling led the Saudis to seek assistance from the Russians, who apparently shipped some HEU to both Iran and Saudi Arabia which augmented what they had purchased from the Pakis and the Chinese. 3) Saudi Arabia has sought the protection of an existing nuclear nation. With the distancing relationship with America, that nation has become the Russian Federation. 4) The Kingdom became thoroughly disenchanted with the Americans' and Europeans' lack of parity and inattention to the Israeli nuclear proliferation, and less than perfectly pleased with the Russians' efforts to supply them. Using its purchases and its enormous financial power, Saudi Arabia has simply been buying nucs. As strange as it may seem, they are trading back their stockpiles of enriched uranium in return for finished bombs. They are nuclear weapon capable, and they are lying about it."

"The Russians? Chinese? Pakistanis?" the incredulous president queried.

"We can't be sure, Sir. Maybe all of them."

"Any thoughts about targets?"

"We don't think they have long range missile capability, but they almost certainly have short and mid-range capability. They are religious fanatics, but they are not as crazy and heedless of danger to themselves as the Iranians. So, the most likely conclusion is that either or both Iran or Israel are the most likely. They certainly hate them both. They have nothing good to say about the Indians and their nucs, but they would have nothing to gain and everything to lose by attacking India."

President Willets scanned the faces of the directors present in the Oval Office for a moment.

"Well," he said, "seems we have some decisions to make."

Chapter Three

Cerisse Daniels was about to have her 17th birthday party and to make a serious announcement. Cerisse was the daughter of billionaire global agri-business mogul and his famous wife, Sybil Norcroft, M.D., Ph.D., F.A.C.S. Cerisse's life started as a slave and deteriorated into sexual slavery in the DRC [Democratic Republic of the Congo]. Her birthdate was unknown, and her mother simply made a best estimate. The girl is a pygmy—a much abused sub-culture in the Congo—whose life was saved by her intrepid mother who was doing a story for Wolf News Network at the time. Cerisse had very little formal schooling, love, positive attention, or possessions before she came into the Daniels family. She was a remarkable child who blossomed dramatically when she entered life in affluent Georgetown with a fully supportive, loving, and protective family. She was given special permission to matriculate in the venerable and very exclusive Georgetown Visitation Preparatory School because her parents were persuasive and generous—donating two million dollars to the scholarship fund. Special tutors put her on a fast track from remedial first grader—at age 13—to successful and competitive senior student in the prestigious school. She was slated to be chosen as the valedictorian at graduation if she continued her stellar performance.

Cerisse's father, Charles, was—of necessity—something of a globe trotter. He was a one-third owner and CEO of Argos Daniels Mitzuki Global Company; and his main achievements were his innovative contributions to the development of hardy proteinaceous, high fiber, low glycemic grains and legumes that could survive in harsh cold, wet, and arid climates. Under Charles's adroit and insightful management, the company had garnered a near corner on the market for the valuable agri-business commodities throughout the world's developing countries, including the patenting, manufacture, installation, and maintenance of innovative wells, land clearing, sowing, and harvesting equipment. His daily work consisted of dealing with heads of multi-national corporations, international law firms, heads of state, and agricultural ministries.

Cerisse's mother, Sybil, used the last name she had when she graduated from medical school—Norcroft—for the general and medical public She was content to be Sybil Daniels in her private life. Sybil was beyond famous in the United States and had a rather strong and growing international following. She was the senior medical consultant for Wolf News Channel and had parlayed that status and fame into a sort-of senior statesman level of recognition and acceptance throughout the states and much of the rest of the world. She—like her wealthy husband—traveled extensively as a featured speaker in United Nations, World Health Organization, and regional health symposia and forums. Sybil juggled an incredible schedule of journalism, oration, maintaining her credentials as a practicing neurosurgeon, and an intense secret life.

Sybil Norcroft, M.D., Ph.D., F.A.C.S., neurosurgeon, media star, philanthropist, sophisticate, star in feminist circles, wife, and mother, also had an Ultra-TS/SCI [Top-Secret, Sensitive Compartmentalized Information, i.e. "above Top Secret"] clearance rating with SSBI [Single Scope Background Investigation]. She was a masterful spy whose duties had required her to head up searches for biological terrorists, intelligence world moles, and to infiltrate the computer systems of major Russian government entities. She was a practiced martial artist, linguist, interrogator, analyst, seductress, liar, and killer—a three dimensional woman if ever there was one. Most of that part of her life was a deeply held secret from her husband, child, friends, and work associates.

The birthday party was an unmitigated joy for Cerisse. The girl was filled with the wonder of life once her new world opened up for her. She took none of the marvelous gifts she had been given or the experiences she had enjoyed since becoming an American for granted. As Thoreau put it, she "sucked the marrow out of life". The generous gifts and out-pouring of affection and good wishes were fully appreciated and acknowledged by the diminutive black girl in a white family. However, Cerisse was also a teenager who had survived horrific maltreatment, PTSD, and a major adjustment in life to become a rather stereotypical American girl. Her hormones had reappeared after her earlier sexual abuse and were now as raging as any other healthy red-blooded teen. She was beginning to make the transition from girl to woman and independence, and that set of changes was beginning to wear on her loving parents just as the accompanying changes did on other parents of precocious teenagers around the world.

Cerisse dropped a sort of bomb-shell on her parents as soon as all the rest of the guests had left the family's multi-million dollar townhouse.

"Mama and Daddy, I have something wonderful to tell you."

Charles and Sybil's eyes brightened.

"I have made a definite decision about what I want to do with the rest of my life."

Charles and Sybil's eyes opened like question marks.

"I am not going to college. Instead, I want to marry my wonderful boyfriend, Andy Witcomb, one of the scholarship students at school. He has great plans to travel the world to help develop world peace starting right after graduation. He wants me to go with him. Isn't that great?"

Charles and Sybil's eyes registered consternation which they tried to hide, and they avoided looking at each other.

Sybil spoke first, "How definite are these plans? I mean, like are you planning to get married? Does he have a job or any plans for an education? Is he prepared to support you, keep you safe, give you a decent life while you are gallivanting about the world saving the downtrodden?"

Ever pragmatic and protective Charles asked, "What do you know about his parents and family? What do they do for a living? Where do they live? What do they think about his plans? Do you have any eye to the future—like educating your fine mind, choosing a career, getting married and having children? By the way, does the world tour include him marrying and making an honest woman of you?"

Cerisse responded the way any normal American teenager would. She dissolved into tears.

"I just knew you wouldn't understand. You don't know Andy like I do. So, he has a little juvenile record. So what, I can help him to get over all of that stuff. He told me he would quit all drugs if I go with him. I can't understand why you can't see that?"

She fled the room.

"I can hardly think of anything to say," Sybil said. "Should we move to Utah and change our names and religion or should we send Guido and Luigi to knee-cap the boy and have him adopt a change of attitude and plans?"

She was only barely kidding.

Charles had a moment to think while Cerisse and Sybil were delivering their salvos.

"We can do a little digging. But, I think we should just let it ride for a while. It wasn't that long ago when she wanted to be a CSI, then a spy, then a medical missionary, and most recently a neurosurgeon like her mother. I am hoping that this, too, shall pass away."

"In the meantime, we need to protect her from little things like unwanted pregnancy, STDs, and dropping out of school," Sybil said morosely.

The two parents agreed to hire McGee and Associates whose private investigations firm had worked with Sybil during the hunt for the deep-cover mole. McGee was effective and discreet, if not inexpensive.

"We can make our decisions when McGee gets back to us," Charles said.

Chapter Four

Five extremely rich men used to living in the lap of luxury at the people's expense were always awed to come to Niavaran Palace. The palace complex is rich in history and consists of several buildings and a museum. The main Niavaran Palace—completed in 1968—was the most splendid and primary residence of the departed Shah and the Imperial family until the Iranian Revolution in 1979. The Ali ibn Muhammad Norouzi family used all of the former Shah's homes, and all of them were of surpassing beauty and splendor—the palaces at Lavasanat, Jamshidiyeh Palace, former palace of Ardeshir Zahedi, Feish Ghola Palace, next to the Caspian Sea, and the Vakil Abad Palace in Mashhad with its 300,000 square meters of grounds.

Niavaran Palace was the favorite residence of its current occupant, the SL [Supreme Leader, the Grand Ayatollah, Ali ibn Muhammad Norouzi], in part because it represented the great power of the Iranian leaders, the supreme among them able to dominate the world of Iran from the favorite home of the former powerful Shah. When Ali ibn Muhammad Norouzi walked through its halls and held audiences and met pilgrims there, he was rubbing the arrogant—now dead—Shah's nose in it.

"Welcome, why have you come?" the supreme leader's first wife asked the standard formal question of all applicants who sought an audience with Grand Ayatollah.

"We are going on a pilgrimage, dear Mrs. Norouzi,"

She nodded and admitted them.

"May your pilgrimage be accepted by God."

They walked behind her to the great doors of the Supreme Leader's audience room. The door opened, and several *bazaaris* [businessmen] exited making one more humble bow before they fully left the room. They had each paid the "lease"— 500 million *toumans*, about $500,000 USD, on their guest slot—their twenty minute pilgrimage. It was well worth their time and contribution, because even a nod from the chief of staff or especially from the Supreme Leader himself, would result in a ten-fold return on their pilgrimage investment.

Hosseini Jahanbani, Norouzi's chief of staff, and a significant imam—a man possessing a divine wisdom, and esoteric knowledge, called *Hikmah*—himself, held the door for them and asked the five men again, "Why have you come?"

Again the five new supplicants bowed slightly and replied, "We are going on a pilgrimage."

No one in Agha Norouzi's office is allowed to say he is going to meet Mr. Norouzi or has a meeting with him. It is not reverential.

"Be humble and mindful today, gentlemen. The Agha was disturbed to learn this morning of the arrest of the witches, jinns, and magicians operating within the army. He recognized that this could have threatened his very person. Fortunately for us all, those demons have all been executed," Jahanbani told them quietly. "You may enter."

None of the five was anyone's fool, and they were right on time. The SL considered anyone who had the audacity to arrive tardy to a meeting with the holiest man in Islam to be a fool. They were Saeed Abdullahi, President of the Republic of Iran; Pirooz ibn Rahmani, Chief of Staff of the Armed Forces of the Republic of Iran; Kourosh Kashani, head of AEOI [the Atomic Energy Organization of Iran]; Mullah, Ali Moqtada Tabatabaei, director of MOIS [The Ministry of Intelligence and Security]; and Hamid Yousefi, director of (MISIRI) or VEVAK, as it is better known [The Ministry of Intelligence and National Security of the Islamic Republic of Iran].

Seated on a replica of the jewel encrusted Peacock throne—symbol of the power of the Shah, and believed by many to have been stolen from India—Agha Norouzi gestured for the men to come forward. His taciturn face gave no hint of his mood of the day; it was as hard as the obsidian and as topographical as the sands of the desert of his country.

"Your report to the intelligence services was well written and to the point, Director Tabatabaei, and your subject is one I find of critical importance to the republic. Please proceed."

"Yes, Agha. Thank you for accepting our pilgrimage."

The SL gave a slight nod.

"Because of provocations from the polytheists in India, our Pakistani brothers in Islam began to focus on the growing threat posed by the Zionist Entity and has kept its eyes on them for twenty years. Although we know for a fact that they have nuclear weapons and the capacity to launch them against us, they have been held in check by the Great Satan. Until this week. While we have, of course, been aware of the unIslamic enmity the lap dog of the Great Satan, Saudi Arabia holds for us, we were lulled into complacency by the protests of the Sauds and the Wahhabs that the Sunni Kingdom had neither nuclear weapon intentions nor capacity.

"They have always maintained that they do not have a nuclear weapons materials production system. To us in the Middle-East, they say that they have been under far too much scrutiny from our intelligence services in the IRI [Islamic Republic of Iran] or the IAEA [International Atomic Energy Agency] to have missed such production facilities. Officially and publicly, the Kingdom is opposed to nuclear weapons within its borders or anywhere else in the Middle-East. The Saudis are signatories of the Nuclear Non-Proliferation Treaty. The Kingdom is a strong member of the coalition of countries demanding a Nuclear-Weapon-Free Zone in the Middle East, and is very public and vocal about it. Official U.N. and our own intelligence services' studies of nuclear proliferation have not identified Saudi Arabia as a country of concern until this week. They are not on any restrictions lists of the United States."

"And what has changed, Director?" Agha Norouzi asked.

"At great risk to his life, our deep-cover agent within the small circle of movers and shakers—as the Americans like to say—has learned that the nasty old Shi'i attacker Muhammad al Saud ibn Wahhab, has been able to purchase live bombs from the *kaffir* Chinese and Russians in exchange for massive amounts of money, crude oil, and transfer of the Saudi stockpile of HEU."

"What is HEU?"

"Highly enriched uranium—weapons quality fissionary fuel."

"That is neither necessarily surprising or alarming. The Sunnis lie through their teeth. We all know that. They hate us and wish our destruction. Perhaps, they only have in mind posing a threat to the Little Satan. They might even launch a nuclear attack and remove that loathsome little backwater country from the map. That would be good riddance for the lice and fleas of the Zionist Entity."

"I regret to report, Agha; but during a meeting in the Royal Clock Tower Hotel in Mecca—where the traitors to Islam have desecrated the holy shrine—ibn Wahhab began to lay out a plan that included a pre-emptive thermonuclear strike against Tehran. Our agents have confirmed the increased electronic message traffic among certain elements of the Saudi government bureaucracy and the intelligence services that confirm our suspicions. I waited until we had what we consider to be adequate indication for concern before bringing the matter to you, your Holiness, knowing how overwhelming the burdens of office and from God that you bear for us."

"This is regrettable. That people of what should be the one true religion should be so divided that those whose concepts are so erroneous should become desperate enough to consider an attack so inspired by Shaytan through the Wahhabis and *Takfiris* [pejorative term for Sunni]. Obviously, we must keep this information in the strictest confidence and begin to make the decisions that the One True God would have us do."

Private Office of the President of Israel, No. 3 Hanassi Street, Jerusalem, Israel, December 18, 2013, 1035 hrs. Present: President Levi Menacham Cohen; Prime Minister Barack Har-Segor, Chief of the *Rav Aluf* [General Staff] of

the IDF; Lieutenant General Moshe Even-Zahav; Director of Mossad, Elad Ben-Zion.
Re: Mossad request for a meeting of the officers of the highest rank holding top-secret clearance ratings.

Unlike many presidential offices around the world, the residence and office of the president of Israel was designed to be a rather simple and humble home. It sits on a low-level rise in the center of Jerusalem. Despite its unassuming appearance, it was designed from the beginning to be secure and to fill all of the functions of the presidential office. The leaders of Israel at the time required of the architects that the presidential offices be true to the emblem of the presidency—a simple Menorah flanked on both sides by olive branches on a blue background.

President Cohen himself invited his three most highly regarded confidants into his cluttered office. He was famous for his filing system, one unique to him and which would pitch the nation into chaos if he were to be incapacitated.

"Gentlemen, have a seat. Care for some tea and cookies? They're Kedem tea biscuits—my favorites—and they're kosher."

President Cohen was the only one in the room who kept kosher, but the purity of his Jewishness and dedication to Israel was infectious. The president poured the tea himself and served the biscuits from a plain white plate with two chips on its edge, an unaffectedly humble gesture. Before the serious discussion began, he passed around a plate of Zelda's gourmet kosher chocolates.

The president was the smallest man in the room, had wiry and attention grasping grey hair that was as unruly as his filing system. In the press he was affectionately referred to as "Einstein" because of the board straight hair that stood up from his head and could not be tamed. His face was old, but his eyes were not. They were grey and clear, and no one ever won a staring contest with the iron-willed man. He had a history in the IDF and Mossad that guaranteed him respect among those who mattered.

He nodded to Director Ben-Zion.

"Mr. President, as usual, I am the bearer of bad tidings; so, I'll come right to the point. Our agent in Saudi Arabia—who has never failed to provide good intel—communicated to the Institute [Mossad] via our most secure network. That, alone, underscores how seriously the agent takes what he has forwarded. In brief, there is a faction in the Kingdom that is actively planning to attack the Motherland. Contrary to what our American cousins and the rest of the world seem to think, the Saudis have full nuclear capability. Our agent thinks that the possession of nuclear warheads is a secret even in the rest of the government. You may have heard of a far-out Wahhabi jihadist named Muhammad al Saud ibn Wahhab. He is reputed to be the master-mind and controller of the WMD program and is known to be a completely ruthless autocrat. We at the Institute consider the information and the threat to be entirely credible, Sir."

There was a moment of contemplative silence. Ben-Zion was a mountain of a man; he remained as formidable opponent in Krav Maga as he was in chess. At sixty, he was still able to bench press 300 pounds, and he had no takers when he made an arm-wrestling challenge. He had short-cropped hair and a craggy face from his long hours spent in the Negev sun during Israel's many wars. He was not ambitious. He was completely loyal to his spy agency and the Nation of Israel; and he never hedged the truth. What he told the other three most powerful men in the country was accepted at full-face value.

Gen. Even-Zahav broke the silence, "Mr. President... Barack...Elad, we are obviously faced with a typical Israeli problem. As always, the questions are should we wait for our American cousins or the United Nations or public opinion before we act? Should we allow the Saudis to take the first offensive step and then return the offense seven times over? Should we wait and see—maybe it will blow over? Should we hope and pray and wait for Jehovah to part the sea or to provide the manna necessary to see us through this modern crisis? Or...should we launch a pre-emptive strike?"

Gen. Even-Zahav was better when he was dealing with his subordinates and could issue orders which had to be followed. He always felt himself to be out of his element when he had to discuss and when he had to submit to the will of a group of civilians, even the president alone. He towered over President Cohen but felt inadequate when he was in the president's office. Even-Zahav was tall, thin, and patrician. He came from money and had an advanced degree—a Ph.D. in nuclear engineering—and was the only one in the room who did. Usually, when he wanted someone to do his bidding, he stretched himself up to his full 6"6' height, gave his underling a withering gaze from his hard brown eyes, and spoke softly. He enjoyed seeing his junior officers quail. None of that could take place in this office. He was uncomfortable with that since what had to be done was so obvious. He held his piece.

President Cohen asked the next questions, "Are we capable of launching a strike into the heartland of Saudi Arabia? Would it be a suicide mission with our brave pilots and crews lacking sufficient fuel to return to Israel? Would the U.S. oppose us? After all, they regard the Kingdom to be tried and true Middle-Eastern regional friends. Give me suggestions to ponder, then I will have decisions to make."

Chapter Five

E rin Novak, the president's secretary, ushered Sybil into the Oval Office.

"Sybil Norcroft, Mr. President. You have five minutes," she announced.

"Sorry this has to be so brief, Sybil; but something is brewing, and I am going to have to make some serious and potentially far-reaching decisions by the end of the day. I hope you understand."

"Certainly, Mr. President. I serve at your pleasure."

"Getting right to it then, Sybil. As you are almost certainly aware, our esteemed Surgeon General, Milton Armstrong, is set to retire in ten days. I have a very short list of candidates for the position; and, frankly, I will choose you if you will accept. I don't want to have it leak that I have already made a choice or that I did not consider the other excellent physician candidates on the list—the list of four as of today.

"I realize that you have conflicts about such a choice. You have already given up a remarkably successful career as a practicing neurosurgeon and academician. You are a media star with Wolf News which is a substantive position beyond the attendant fame. I can't get around it; you would have to give up that career as well. The job I am offering will likely dim your fame and certainly will decrease your annual income. It is an often thankless and not very exciting position; but, in my perception, an important one. Getting down to brass tacks, I need you to continue your secret life as a special agent of the CIA and to accept the Surgeon General position; so, you can get into places that unofficial Sybil Norcroft, M.D., Ph.D., F.A.C.S. and media celebrity cannot. From time to time, you can render invaluable service to the country and to me."

"This is not the first time you have suggested this appointment, Mr. President; but it is the most definitive request. You are right about all of my entanglements; and, if truth be known, about my ambitions. I want to make a contribution. I don't need money; that does not enter the equation. I guess I fear that becoming the Surgeon General—as lofty a position as it is—would be the end of my rise. I hate that that makes me sound like the quintessential Washington insider, but the truth is often not entirely palatable."

"How about if I sweeten the pot, Madam hard negotiator?" the president laughed.

"Well, Sir, make me an offer I can't refuse," Sybil answered and smiled broadly and genuinely.

She liked the man, and he knew it. They had a history together and were mutually respectful. He realized that there was nothing sycophantic about her; and, indeed, she probably would have more to offer as time wore on. She would be a better candidate for him to foster than many of the suck-ups he had to deal with. It took him no time to make a larger offer.

"Sybil, I have been thinking about this for some time, actually. Martin Edelweiss will retire in three years. I would like to give his DDCIA [Deputy Director of the CIA] Andrew Dillon a chance to serve as the DCIA for his last tour of duty for the government. He has made the unusual request of me—the first request of his stellar forty-year career—that he be allowed to serve one year and then to retire with that as the final achievement in his curriculum vitae. I would like to have you accept the directorship as his successor. That would be in 2019. I will still be in office, and I consider my word to be my bond. Do you trust me enough to accept the Surgeon General's slot until then?"

"Wow, that's a bit of a shock. What can I say? Yes, sir, I do trust you; and I accept."

"Thanks. I'll announce your appointment four days from now. You will need to wind up your affairs at Wolf News, but your CIA status will remain unchanged…and secret. Sorry, I have to get on to the rest of this day."

That was an obvious signal that the interview was over. To punctuate that fact, Erin Novak quietly slipped into the Office and announced that the Foreign Minister of Saudi Arabia and Thompson Kennedy, the Secretary of State, were outside.

Wolf News Headquarters, Avenue of the Americas in New York, December 28, 2015, 1000 hrs
Present: Gerard Montpelier, President; Sybil Norcroft-Daniels, Senior Medical Consultant; David Kilcannon,

Vice-President of Production; and Gwen Packard, Vice-President for human resources.

Sybil got right to the point, "I have some news—good or bad, depending on how you look at it. President Willets asked me to come to the Oval Office a week ago to offer me the position of Surgeon General."

"Seriously!?" Gwen exclaimed.

None of the Wolf News personnel could have seen that coming.

"And...?" asked David.

"I took a week. There was a serious timeline on the president's part. I said, 'yes'."

"When will the appointment become effective?" President Montpelier asked.

"I will go to the White House this afternoon for the formal announcement. Technically, the reins of office won't be transferred for another two weeks. The Surgeon General has told the president that I should have at least that long to learn the ropes anyway. As I see it, I can spend most of my time here clearing up loose ends like the spousal abuse series and the forum program at the U.N. with Raza Patel, the director general of the World Health Organization, and I discussing how to achieve global economy in healthcare delivery for developing and third-world countries.

"WWN and Wolf will alternate evenings with two hours on two nights each—a full eight hours. We have bio-medical engineers, humanitarians, Doctors Without Borders, economists, and some fascinating time and motion experts who will round out the programs. Dr. Patel and I will narrate for our respective channels. I will stay mornings in D.C. with Dr. Armstrong; so, he can bring me up to speed. I hope that will give you enough time to find a replacement for me. I certainly will always want to continue our cordial relationship."

"We would be nuts to do anything else, Sybil. You know that. You would likely be a bad enemy. And, we can milk the publicity that will gather around your new appointment for all it's worth. Wolf News consultant makes good...And look, here she is to give us an exclusive interview. 'How nice it is to see you back in the studios, Gen. Norcroft. What is your breaking news that will air here on Wolf exclusively?"

They all had a good laugh at Kilcannon's chutzpah.

At three p.m., Sybil and two other people were gathered in the White House Briefing Room for a televised taping of the announcements of their appointments which would be aired on prime-time news later that evening. The announcements were brief and to the point but full of praise for the new government officials.

President Willets invited Sybil to the podium.

"Today I am pleased to announce the appointment of Doctor Sybil Norcroft to be the next Surgeon General of the United States. She will be replacing our beloved Milton Armstrong who has served so faithfully and well in the position for the past four years. We wish General Armstrong every happiness as he heads into his well-earned retirement.

"Dr. Norcroft is a Doctor of Medicine from Duke University and a Doctor of Philosophy from the University of Texas specializing in neurophysiology. She survived the arduous training program in neurosurgery at UCLA. She has had a long and distinguished career in private practice and in academic medicine. Until recently she has been a significant media personality making contributions on a host of medical issues and has helped represent the United States in a number of foreign countries to help the less fortunate.

She is the recipient of a number of awards which attest to her accomplishments. I, personally, have been witness to her help in the recent Marburg virus epidemic. She is a forceful and dedicated servant of the people of the United States. I have every confidence that she will continue to be a major asset as she assumes the mantel of Surgeon General."

The other two nominees were John Breckhouse and Madeleine Sharkowski who were slated to become ambassadors to New Zealand and Ethiopia respectively. All three nominees would have to undergo the Senate advice and consent process before their appointments were confirmed. The nominees were all expected to sweep through the vetting process as a quick pro forma experience. That would prove to be true for Ambassadors-Elect Breckhouse and Sharkowski.

Wisconsin Avenue, NW, Georgetown, Washington D.C., December 28, 2015, 1900 hrs.

As always, Sybil loved coming home and being away from the excitement of Wolf News, the labyrinthine politics of Washington D.C., and the angst of being a spy. Above all, she loved to share the unimportant important family trivia with Charles and Cerisse.

"I want to hear about each of your days. Okay if we start with you, Cerisse?" Sybil said working to restrain her enthusiasm for announcing her new career.

Charles could read his wife very easily and knew when she was up to something, and this was one of those times. He had some intel of his own.

Cerisse was grumpy.

"I had a regular day—math, science, statistics, English, art history, and soccer—same old stuff. Boring. But I did get to spend some time with Andy. Quality time," she said with undue emphasis. "I don't get to see him very much anymore, and it makes me mad."

"*Maybe that's because he dropped out of school along with dropping out of life,*" Charles said silently to himself working diligently to keep his thoughts from showing through on his face.

"Anything else, Cerisse?" Sybil asked innocently.

She knew what Charles was going to report and had some trepidations about how that would go over.

"Your turn, Daddy," she said.

Charles opened a manila folder and looked at Cerisse soberly but with as much kindness as he could muster under the circumstances.

"Cerisse, your mother and I have been trying to find about something more about your friend, Andy. During our last conversation, it appeared that you didn't really know very much, and that you were perhaps a little too hasty to defend some of the elements of his record that you did know about."

"You've been checking up on my friends?! My boyfriend?!" shrieked Cerisse, the first time she had ever raised her voice to her adoptive parents; and the only time she had been seriously critical of them.

"Yes. Our most important job is to protect you, Cerisse. You know that. We have worked at that since your mama first saw you there in the jungle looking at your dead friends and family," Charles said calmly.

Sybil was well aware of the dirt that McGee & Associates, Investigators had found with more than a little help from her own CIA and local police connections.

"So, what is so awful?!" Cerisse demanded to know.

"Come and sit by me on the couch, and I'll show you what your mama and I have learned."

It took Cerisse ten minutes to read everything in the folder. She was not experienced enough to realize that she was looking at Andy's juvenile criminal records—his sealed records—and at photographs taken by the private investigation firm of Andy in compromising situations, not the least of which was of him with a group of what appeared to be hippies. The photos were all time stamped and recent. He was kissing and embracing two of the girls in their skimpy tie-dye blouses and short-shorts. In several of the shots he was smoking funny-looking cigarettes; and in one, he was shooting up with the help of an older man who was seen reaching into a black doctor's bag for supplies.

The teenager was stricken. Nothing had to be said by her parents. The photographs spoke volumes for themselves. She burst into tears and walked sadly out of the room.

Sybil said, "We should go after her and comfort her. This is terrible. I feel so guilty."

Charles differed, "Let's leave her alone. She's smart, and she's tough. Let her work it all out for herself."

It was anti-climactic when Sybil announced to Charles about her impending selection to be the next Surgeon General of the United States. She held off on any premature announcement about the potential for her to become the Director of the Central Intelligence Agency someday. She planned to tell Cerisse about the Surgeon General appointment in the morning when she was in a better frame of mind.

Chapter Six

**Dirksen Senate Office Building, Hearing Room 538,
Washington, D.C., January 4, 2016, 1000 to 1600 hrs.
United States Senate Executive Session to consider the
nomination of Dr. Sybil Norcroft of Massachusetts, to be
the Surgeon General of the United States.
Present: A quorum of the committee and Dr. Norcroft**

Chairman: Before the committee is the nomination of Sybil
Norcroft, M.D., F.A.C.S. to be the Surgeon General of the
United States. Does everyone have the administration's brief
on the doctor?

The committee responded unanimously in the affirmative.

Chairman: Any questions about the documents?"

The committee responded unanimously in the negative.

Chairman: The committee calls Dr. Norcroft. Good morning,
Doctor. Thank you for coming.

Dr. Norcroft: I appreciate the privilege.

Chairman: The chair retains its privilege to question later.
The floor is now open for questions from the committee

members. We will go from left to right as we face the room. Mr. Delancy.

Mr. Delancy: Good morning, Doctor, I am Reginald Delancy from the great state of California. Welcome.

Dr. Norcroft: Thank you.

Mr. Delancy: I have a few questions about your background. I find one disturbing area which is given very short shrift in the administration's brief. Tell us, if you will, about your having been indicted for murder, kidnapping, and grand theft. The incidents occurred in my fine state; so, it is incumbent on me to get to the truth of the matter and how that impinges on your character and the appropriateness of you becoming the Surgeon General of these great United States.

Sybil spoke for thirty minutes on the subject, emphasizing the not-guilty verdict and the apology from the court. She also called the committee's attention to the fact that another defendant was arrested, tried, found guilty, and is now serving a life sentence without the possibility of parole in Folsom State Prison.

Ms. Haight: Have you had any other criminal proceedings against you, Doctor?

Dr. Norcroft: No.

Mr. Nicholsen: I only have a comment and that is to express the profound gratitude of the people of the great state of Maryland for your work in identifying and helping to eradicate the terrible pestilence of the Marberry Plague.

Dr. Norcroft: Thank you. But for the record it was the Marburg Hemorrhagic Fever Virus Epidemic.

Mr. Greyson: Madam, I am Kendell Grayson, a proud son of the great state of Kansas. I am informed that you are a supporter of several abominations. Among them are lesbian, gay, bisexual, and transsexual sinners, the heinous malfeasance of gay marriage, the ungodly and unbiblical concept that men came from monkeys, and of the legalized murder of unborn children. Is that not so?

Dr. Norcroft: I am a supporter of minority peoples including feminists which you did not mention. I do support same-sex marriage. I oppose abortion except in the most extreme instances, but in any governmental position, I am constrained to recognize that it is the law of the land that a woman may have an abortion in a clean, safe facility.

I believe in science and the scientific method. In that regard, the Darwinian theory of evolution is a well-qualified scientific theory, i.e. by strict definition, a coherent and well documented and established set of generalized propositions used as principles of explanation of a class of phenomena. Evolution is strictly confined to natural biological phenomena and has nothing to do with the supernatural.

Mr. Greyson: I take it then that you do not believe in the supernatural or the bible or God or any of the traditions that make this country great.

Chair: Caution, Mr. Greyson, your questions are bordering on the inflammatory and have very questionable relationship to the office for which Dr. Norcroft is nominated.

Mr. Greyson: I beg to differ, sir. You on the left may accept these attacks on the very fiber of our nation, but we proud conservatives cannot let these things just pass. Can a person who holds such views be responsible for the health of our citizens, especially our impressionable young?

Chair: Your time is nearly up. How about one more question for the nominee.

Mr. Greyson: Tell us your view of man's origins and why you accept a godless atheistic alternative to the Holy Writ?

Dr. Norcroft: I am a church going Episcopalian. I am also a scientist. As a physician and a student of the real world of biology, I, like my scientist colleagues, am bound to deal with the working value of Darwin's theory. Perhaps it would be worthwhile to give a very brief sketch of some of the important aspects of evolution:

Darwin's theory of natural selection entails two main aspects, namely, that:

1. organisms produce offspring with at least some heritable variation, and,
2. and organisms generally produce more offspring than their environment is able to sustain.

At its simplest, Darwin's theory—with the refinements of 150 years of study, includes, even requires—six basic components:

1. Evolution
2. Gradualism
3. Speciation
4. Common ancestry
5. Natural selection, and
6. Nonselective mechanisms of evolutionary change

Given these two fundamental aspects and the six basic components, some variants are necessarily fitter than others in the sense that their offspring are more likely to survive in an environment and from environmental changes and produce a next generation of offspring. It follows that a species undergoes genetic change over time. Darwin proposed that such changes were generally small, sporadic, incremental, and required extremely long periods of time to manifest themselves for the most part—a process labeled gradualism. The result is the development of new species by splitting—speciation. Looking in reverse, the development of new species implies that there was an ancestral species, a single or few common ancestors. Darwin's most remarkable contribution to the world of natural science and to biology, and certainly his most controversial idea, was the concept of natural selection. That concept gives a purely materialistic explanation of what otherwise appears to be explainable only by invoking a Creator or Intelligent Designer. At its simplest, natural selection acts on populations with the capacity to alter their genetic makeup and thereby to reproduce more successfully in a given environment. Reproductive capacity is the key to natural selection and to evolution.

Chair: Mr. Greyson, I think the subject of science, evolution, religion, and far-right political philosophy has been exhausted.

Mr. Greyson: Mock me if you will, but this godlessness will bring down our God protected country. I will yield the floor now, but I will never vote in favor of a godless one being a part of our fine federal government.

Ms Toraulf: Doctor Norcroft, could you tell us your political views and how they might impinge on your work as the Surgeon General. After all, you would certainly have a bully pulpit to sell your views.

Dr. Norcroft: I am a political independent. I am more concerned about issues than party politics or party officialdom. I do not and will not have a political agenda if you do me the great favor of affirming my nomination. I will strongly advocate for scientific, evidence-based medical principles, and will do my very best to educate and to protect the safety and health of the people of the United States.

Mr. Randall: I understand that you hate football. Say it is not so to a humble senator from the great State of Texas where football is as much a part of the American way as apple pie and vanilla ice-cream.

Dr. Norcroft: The record is replete with evidence of what I think about football. You can look up the archives of Wolf News and WWN and see what Dr. Raza Patel and I have said and upon what evidence our statements were made. No, I don't hate football. I do hate the terrible injuries that occur in that game, and I am very much concerned about the inordinate financial drain on our school systems that football requires.

Seven days later the committee voted 9 to 8 with 3 abstentions in favor of sending the nomination to the floor. In the afternoon, the Senate voted with a slight majority of 61 to confirm Sybil Norcroft as the Surgeon General.

The president's chief of staff caught Sybil as she left the Senate gallery after being confirmed and asked her to meet with the president as soon as the two of them could get to the Oval Office.

"Thank you for coming, Sybil. You no doubt know the Director of the CIA, Mr. Edelweiss."

"I do. Good afternoon, Director."

"We will make your confirmation big news on all of the media channels tonight because we need to have our esteemed friends in Saudi Arabia aware of your status. The director and I have arranged for you to travel to Al-Ahsa, SA to attend a health care symposium. You will meet an agent who will identify himself as "Donovan", and he will give you instructions and some gear for use in a mission we deem to be of considerable importance. We have chosen the code-name "Miriam" for you. Any problems with getting back into the secrets business?"

"I guess not, Mr. President. I suppose there are things I don't need to know, but one question: will this be wet-work?"

"No...more on the lines of your work in Russia under the "Gideon" project," Director Edelweiss said.

Chapter Seven

The 4th Saudi International Conference on Healthcare Information Technology, (2015), King Saud bin Abdulazziz University for Health Sciences Al-Ahsa Branch, Al-Ahsa, Eastern Province, Saudi Arabia, January 9, 2015, 1900 hrs.

The DCIA had two of Sybil's friends and cooperating agents—Ed Simonsen from the Marburg virus epidemic terrorist attack and Mac Young from the Gideon Affair, the top secret exposure and removal of the traitorous mole in the NCIS—providing all she needed to carry out the espionage assignment for which she was uniquely suited. The healthcare information technology symposium in Al-Ahsa was deadly dull for Sybil who found it very difficult to become interested in the engineering details of the technology. She saw herself as being more like Henry Ford who sued the Chicago Tribune in 1919 for calling him an anarchist. During the trial, the defendant newspaper's attorneys suggested that Ford was stupid, illiterate, and ignorant.

To prove that he was none of those, he took a delegation to his plant and instructed them to ask him a question. Several did, and as answers he signaled one expert or another on his payroll and almost instantly obtained a detailed, erudite, and complete set of responses. That settled the question of whether or not the automobile mogul was ignorant, and the jury verdict in the civil trial was in Ford's favor—he won six cents.

As the Surgeon General of the United States, Sybil was an honored guest; and, although she knew almost nothing about information technology, she was able to communicate convincingly about the crucial value of IT in the delivery of safe, efficient, and efficacious medical care. This was thanks to a speech written for her by CIA researchers in cooperation with premier IT engineers from MIT [Massachusetts Institute of Technology]. The speech was given on the first day and went over well. Otherwise, Sybil had no role to play and was on her own for the next three days of the gathering. Ed, Mac, and four other agents formed a security detail for Sybil, nothing more than was expected for U.S. Army lieutenant general.

Ed and Mac supplied more than security.

After her speech, Ed slipped up to her and said, "I'm Donovan in case you haven't already guessed."

"And I'm Miriam," Sybil said, "but you know that. It makes the game more fun though."

He gave her a small USB flash drive containing information in the form of a highly sophisticated computer virus. It was not necessary for Sybil to understand the flash drive or what it contained. She simply had to install the information into certain computers belonging to the Saudi Air Force Missile Command. Those computers resided in a highly secure facility just outside the great oasis of Al-Ahsa. It was understandably quite tricky to get access to the computers. That was what Sybil Norcroft—the spy—brought to the effort; she was accurately known for her ingenious resourcefulness, the humint—and she had the mantle of U.S. officialdom.

With information supplied by the CIA, Sybil sought out the commanding general of the missile facility during the opening night banquet. She bribed the head usher to seat her next to the general and spent an hour and a half in scintillating conversation with the arrogant air force officer. She was witty, charming, and interested—both in the man's work and accomplishments but also in him—and she was not shy about using almost all of the weapons in her feminine armamentarium—sloe-eyed looks, batting eyelashes, laughing at his corny and mostly off-color jokes, and a liberal dose of flattery. Her efforts worked.

"Would you like to have a guided tour of my facility, my dear?" Gen. ibn Muhammad asked as dessert was being served.

"*I thought you would never ask,*" Sybil thought.

She said, "I would be delighted."

"I will be free tomorrow afternoon, would that be a convenient time, General Norcroft?"

"Perfect. Would it be proper for me to dress in a jump suit as protection against the sand storms that I understand are so prevalent as one gets closer to the *Rub' al Khali* [Empty Quarter] desert."

"Of course, my dear. Since you are not a Muslim, the restrictions on wearing apparel do not apply. It will be more suitable if you are covered by a garment that prevents exposure of your neck, wrists, and ankles and that you wear a head scarf. You know men, I am sure. Out here they are away from their wives, and their minds can wander at the sight of a well-turned ankle. I am sure you understand."

"Certainly. Neither I nor my country would care to embarrass you or your traditions. Thank you for the fascinating conversation, General. I will look forward with enthusiasm to the visit," Sybil said with a hint of invitation in her voice.

"Will you need transportation?"

"No, my security detail will take me out to the facility. Thank you, anyway."

Ed and Mac came to Sybil's hotel room late that evening with news from the Company.

Mac said, "The DDCIA sent us a message. The DUSCYBERCOM [Director U.S. Cyber Command] and DCIA-CT [Director CIA-Counter Terrorism] have discovered the existence of a missile site in the *Rub' al Khali* not far from the official air force missile facility. That empty quarter site is not on any map, and the Kingdom does not admit to its existence. We need to get a close look at it. Do you think we could return to Al-Ahsa by way of the *Rub' al Khali* tomorrow? We have GPS coordinates."

"Something like a little detour—one that heads off in the opposite direction of the oasis, perhaps?" Sybil asked with a knowing smile.

"Something like that," Mac said.

Ed added, "The DCIA-CT also informed us of another little Saudi secret or maybe it is only a Saudi faction secret. The Saudis have entered into a contract with the CNNC [China National Nuclear Corporation] and a French company nobody ever heard of called Systèmes de Missiles de France and the Pakistan Atomic Energy Commission. While it is well advertised that Saudi Arabia plans to construct sixteen nuclear power reactors over the next 20 years at a cost of more than $80 billion, there is no information that suggests that any of them are planned for the site in the *Rub' al Khali* for which the CIA has GPS coordinates that we have found or that any one of the plants is operational yet. It would appear that something is afoot, as Shakespeare would say; and we should have a look."

"That's enough to make anyone nervous. Any idea about who the Saudis might be targeting?" Sybil asked.

"Above our pay-grade;" Mac told her, "and, apparently, we don't need to know."

"Fair enough. Let's see if we can make it happen tomorrow, then."

The Eastern Province is the largest province of Saudi Arabia. The current governor of the province is His Royal Highness Prince Saud Sultan Sharif ibn Abu Bakr, which is indicative of the importance assigned to the large, largely arid desert province. Al-Ahsa city is an oasis about 37 miles inland from the Persian Gulf. The oasis is the largest in the world and lies as an island in a great sea of ever-shifting barren sand. The oasis has an estimated three million date palms, reputedly the best in the world.

In addition, Al-Ahsa is one of the very few areas in Saudi Arabia wet enough for growing and exporting rice. Above the value of the dates and the rice, the trees and rice plants make the oasis extraordinarily green and beautiful. Outside the oasis, the huge Eastern Province is the location of most of Saudi Arabia's oil production which makes the region very busy. Remarkably, the rich Eastern Province is also home to the largest concentration of Twelvers [Shi'ite Muslims] in the very predominantly Sunni Muslim country. That fact would become important for the world of espionage after Sybil and her CIA entourage had their visit.

It was hot when Sybil's convoy of three HMMWVs [High Mobility Multipurpose Wheeled Vehicles]—fitted with balloon tires for soft sand travel—set out for the air force missile facility in the largest sand desert in the world—600 miles long and 310 miles wide—larger than the State of Texas. Daily maximum temperatures average over 115 °F in the Empty Quarter and are known to climb as high as 133 °F. The day chosen for the reconnaissance was one of those days. Before noon, their thermometers recorded 130°. It had been ten years since the last rain. Only the effective air-conditioning of the sophisticated HMMWVs made the trip anywhere near tolerable. In addition to an impressive array of weapons, the eight CIA agents packed 150 gallons of water, 200 gallons of diesel fuel, and enough MREs [Meals Ready to Eat] to last eight adults a week.

It suited the needs of the Saudi air force general to keep the visit secret, and the Sybil had been only too happy to comply. Like most CIA adventures, this was going to be one that never happened.

Chapter Eight

Gen. Abdullah ibn Muhammad and his three aides-de-camp met Sybil, Mac, Ed, and their five security officers at the front gate of the fortress King Achmed Air Force Missile Base. The general was effusive, and the aides were obsequious.

"Welcome, welcome. Col. Nadhir will escort the security personnel on a tour of the base facilities outside the main operational center. Col. Samaha, Major Rahal, and I will show the Surgeon General our sophisticated information systems. It should be quite enlightening after the fine lectures regarding IT we heard yesterday in the symposium. I'm afraid we cannot take any of you to see the actual missile silos—security, of course. I am sure you understand."

"Of course," Sybil said.

All she really cared about was the chance to get alone with a couple of the important computers. The missile base security guards relieved Sybil and all of her entourage of their weapons and cell phones for the duration of their stay at the King Achmed base.

"I am sure you are perfectly facile with the computers we use here, Gen. Norcroft. They are very much the same as would be found in the lower floors of the Pentagon. We do have some interesting arrays, however. Would you like to see what we have?"

"Very much."

"*It's the only reason I came out here into this God-forsaken oven,*" she thought.

The colonel and the major appeared anxious to get back to their real duties and had to strive to be courteous to the female general—an unthinkable oxymoron in Saudi Arabia. An hour into the lengthy presentation of the arcane qualities of the computer system and its interface with all other computers in the missile service network, Gen. ibn Muhammad was called away to handle a top-level issue in another building.

"Why don't you get Gen. Norcroft a refreshment, Major, and perhaps it would be a good time to take a bathroom break. I won't be long," Gen ibn Muhammad said.

The two remaining air force officers groaned inwardly at the prospect of having to squire the American woman around without the commander. Sybil read their faces and seized on the opportunity their disinterest provided.

"I don't need a refreshment, thank you," she said to the officers, "but I would enjoy a trip to the ladies room and time to sit on a comfortable chair. Perhaps you two would like to take a smoke break?"

She had read their minds. They tried not to show their profound relief.

"Shall we say…fifteen minutes?" the colonel ventured.

"That would be very nice. I'll see you then. Maybe I will take a walk to the kiosk and get a lemonade after all."

The two officers made a bee-line for the exit and the smoking area. They each had the habit bad and were not allowed to smoke inside any of the buildings.

When she could no longer see their backs, Sybil backtracked away from the main second-floor lobby area and headed quickly for the massive computer room. Mac had instructed her about the interconnectivity of the computer array, and how her one 512 gigabyte USB [integrated Universal Serial Bus interface] flash drive could impart its information to almost every computer in the system from just one port. She deftly pushed the extended connector into the USB port on the first mega-computer in the line which stretched fifty yards along the huge room. Now came the sweat. Mac had cautioned her to be patient. It was crucial to allow a full five minutes for the flash drive to do what it was engineered to do. That was what Sybil did not need to know.

She fidgeted and squirmed as the time crept by with glacial celerity. At the two minute mark, two security guards walking their rounds came into Sybil's peripheral vision. She had no choice but to leave the flash drive in place and to walk nonchalantly out of the computer area and around the corner to the ladies room. She had been so intent on what she was doing that she had not paid attention to the signals from her bladder. So, the trip was not a waste.

At the four minute mark, she exited the lavatory and cautiously walked back to the computer room. The room was very cool and occasionally staff personnel moved in and out of the area just to enjoy the air conditioning. No one paid any attention to her. With fifteen seconds to go, she screwed up her courage and moved to the computer with its protruding flash drive. At five minutes and two seconds, she whisked the flash drive out of its port and into her pocket so quickly that no one who was not specifically assigned to follow her could have noticed. She gave a quick sigh and began to work on her limbic system to tone done her anxiety.

Sybil then moved quickly out of the room and walked to the kiosk where an attendant gave her two paper cups full of lemonade. She was holding those cups when her two minders returned.

"Did you enjoy your lemonade, General?" Major Rahal asked.

"I did, thank you. It was refreshing. Do we expect Gen. ibn Muhammad to return soon?" she asked.

"I'm afraid not. He called to let us know that he would be detained for the rest of the day and sends his regrets."

"A pity," she said, speaking Arabic to them." Well, gentlemen, I don't need to keep you any longer. You and your government have been most hospitable. Although I don't understand a thing about all of the tech equipment, it is truly remarkable what you have accomplished here. In fact, I am most impressed with what the Kingdom has accomplished; you have made the desert blossom like a rose."

She cautioned herself to damp down the flattering rhetoric before they became suspicious. She need not have exercised herself. Arabic is a flowery mellifluous language, and she was only talking the way a native speaker would express herself. The two men were surprised to hear the language of Allah and His Prophet—may his memory remain in the minds of men forever—come from the mouth of an infidel. They were pleased, but not nearly as pleased as they were at the prospect of getting rid of her. She was too attractive for comfort.

Sybil met Ed, Mac, and the body guards at the entrance to the headquarters building and together they walked into the parking lot and got into their convey HMMWVs and exited the compound. They turned back in the direction of Al-Ahsa until they were certain that they were out of sight. Then they made a 180° turn into the desert and set their GPSs for the site of the covert facility near the Yemeni border.

Covert Saudi Nuclear Storage and Missile Facility Somewhere Else in the *Rub' al Khali*, near the Northern Border with Yemen, January 10-12, 2016

The convoy wound around ever shifting sand dunes. Everyone knew that without the GPS they could well become statistics and just another small military squad lost in the vastness. The GPS told them that they were getting close—too close; so, they found an especially large dune and stopped behind it to eat. The plan was to wait until dark before venturing up close to the buildings. They could not yet be sure what the level of security was going to be.

Sybil was totally surprised when—almost immediately after the sun went down and turned the earth to black—the temperature dropped to below freezing. The penetrating cold wind made it feel more like 0° F.

Nick Haggerty, one of the security guards and an old desert hand, said, simply, "*Hawa*" [the wind].

It blew in with a vengeance bringing with it grit that made it feel like one was being sand-papered into oblivion. It quickly deteriorated into a choking, swirling, sand blizzard which forced all hands into their tents and to don protective head and face fiber metal shields and long thick cotton *ghutrahs*.

The traditional Arab garment has long folds of fabric, and the CIA agents drew the folds across their faces. The garment has certainly withstood the test of time, having protected all sorts of desert travelers from sandstorms, heat, and the burning sun, for millennia. No other fabric has ever been found that is better than cotton to keep the head and body cool in the hot desert climate.

Hoping not to sound whiny, Sybil asked Nick how long they could expect the wind to last.

He replied somberly, "Some *shamals* [sand bearing winds] from the north have been known to blow for as long as a month before dying down."

"Glad I asked," Sybil muttered.

It was not the worst *shamal* Nick had seen; so, he advised Sybil, Mac, and Ed that they should take advantage of the cover provided by the dense gritty air pollution to get up close to the military site. They were inexperienced; so, they relied on Nick and moved out. The desert camo HMMWVs stayed as close to each other as they could without causing an accident. Visibility was down to less than ten feet.

Sybil was afraid they would stumble right into one of the installations buildings; but their military grade GPSs were accurate to within a few feet; and she need not have worried about that. There were other things to worry about, however.

When the convoy had crept to within fifty yards of what they presumed was the perimeter of the site, they began to see and hear evidence of patrol activity.

"These guys have to be real serious to come out in this crap," Ed said. "Let's park here and hoof it in closer. They could spot the Hummers anytime now."

Sybil wanted to groan, but she did not want to embarrass herself by sounding or acting like a potted begonia.

She braced herself and slipped out of the protective cocoon afforded by the vehicle and into the maelstrom of abrasive wind. She slogged along among the men. It was like walking chest deep in molasses, but she kept up.

It took an hour to go fifty yards, and one of the men swore when he walked into a building. That was sobering. They were almost in the belly of the beast, and the specter of being caught loomed constantly. Ed, Mac, and Sybil huddled together and agreed to hunker down where they were until the wind died down or it got somewhat lighter out; so, they could make a rational decision about what to do next.

Ed whispered hoarsely, "We don't have to be much concerned about camouflage. We and everyone and everything else will all look the same—like piles of light beige sand."

"In the dark, all cats are grey," Mac mused.

They waited. At 0430, there was a conspicuous reduction in the wind and some accompanying visibility. The base muezzin began the call for the *Fajr* [morning prayer] at just after 0500. By 0530—the time approaching pre-dawn early light—they became aware that they were no longer being pelted with the stinging sand and dim images were taking shape.

"Let's go to night vision equipment," Mac said.

The change in the ability to see was dramatic. It was an eerie green world, but vision was quite good. The crew had blundered their way into a small protective alcove, and the passing security trucks could not see them.

"Okay, we won't have much time. Let's divide into two groups—four to the right and four to the left. Each group take a Geiger counter. Synchronize your chronometers and meet back here in twenty minutes, no longer. I have 0534."

Everyone agreed. Sybil, Ed and two security guards went to the right, hugging the sand blasted wall of what proved to be a very large silo. The Geiger counter began an annoying buzzing as they walked along.

"There's a lot of radioactivity here, lady and gentlemen," Ed commented.

"I am a bit worried about my retinae and my thyroid," Sybil said.

Ed nodded his head, "I have a few other worries."

They walked up to the edge of a heavy metal door which was emblazoned with an international radioactive materials sign. There were three large Saudi air force trailer trucks with as many missiles lying on the trailers.

"Sand can't help those missiles to function," Ed commented.

"That can't be a bad thing, I'm thinking," Sybil responded.

Tom Eggerly, one of the two security men with Sybil and Ed, said, "We've been separated for fifteen minutes. We are going to have to make tracks to get back by the twenty minute deadline."

There did not seem to be anything more to gain by lingering; so, the four of them trotted back to the original alcove. The other four were already there.

"See anything?" Sybil asked Mac.

"A truck load of nuclear hazmat suits and a van loaded with shower stalls—looks like they're preparing to wash off nuclear contamination."

Ed said, "We better make like geese and get the flock out of here. It's becoming busy. Our luck can't hold forever. I think we are pretty likely to have to make a run for it. Let's lock and load."

That took two minutes. It was now dangerously light. The sun was peaking over the tall dunes on the east.

"Crawl or run?" Ed asked Mac.

"Much as I want to get out of here, I guess our best chance is to crawl. It's a fur piece back to the Hummers, but I presume it's better to eat sand than bullets."

They began a high crawl which was faster but more conspicuous. Sybil found the going to be difficult because she kept getting tangled up in the long folds of cotton cloth of her *ghutrah*. After twenty yards, a foot patrol from the area of the silo walked between the CIA agents and their HMMWVs.

"On your faces," Mac ordered.

The fine sand wafted up in small choking puffs. It was maddening.

The security patrol passed without seeing their enemies or the HMMWVs.

"Low crawl," Mac ordered when it appeared that they were out of immediate danger.

That mode of movement was exhausting and frustrating. It seemed to be painfully slow; but when another patrol came towards them, the team was able to sink down onto the sand and to appear to be just another few of the many lumps and dunes that had formed during the *shamal*.

"*This is a ridiculous place for a Surgeon General of the United States to be*," Sybil thought.

She could not bring herself to contemplate the horrors for her and the humiliation for the U.S. if she were to get caught. She actively drove thoughts of her daughter, Cerisse, and her husband, Charles, away from her consciousness. She tested the slight irregularity in the second lower molar on the right with her tongue—the tooth with the cyanide. She could not afford to lose focus. Not now.

The patrol passed. It seemed like a miracle—in which Sybil, the scientist, did not believe—that they had not been discovered. By sheer force of will, Sybil was able to keep up with the men until they got to the clutch of vehicles. She thanked The Farm [secret CIA training center in rural Virginia] for the training that had hardened her enough to get through this.

Mac turned over on his back and raised his head for a look. There was another patrol heading their way. If that squad sighted them, they would have to fight their way into the vehicles and make a run for it. The chances were not that great of escaping because they were so close to the buildings of the facility. However, they did have the positive element of surprise on their side. Mac strained to see which put him into what amounted to a very prolonged and intense sit-up. He knew that he was going to have a very sore belly tomorrow. If there was a tomorrow.

He whispered, "Mount up. I don't have to say, 'be quiet'. We're going to have a fight; the only question is when or where. Let's not have it here."

Chapter Nine

The doors to the HMMWVs were built to be quiet upon opening and closing. When there were no security troops in sight, the CIA troops slid into the vehicles. Everyone gritted their teeth as the engines jumped into life. The sound seemed deafening to Sybil; she could not imagine that the security details from the nuclear storage and missile site could miss hearing the engine noises especially now that the wind had died down.

"Move out slow-like," Mac's phone-to-phone transmission whispered, and they began to move.

The convoy avoided the road—an incongruously well-paved thoroughfare—that seemed to go nowhere out into the sand. They moved as cautiously as possible but still needed to create some distance from the military site.

Their encounter with the Saudi military did not result from the sentries at the site hearing or seeing them but; rather, from a chance encounter with a large truck and trailer carrying a missile coming in from the north. The CIA contingent was on an oblique course avoiding the road. The truck seemed to spring out of a sand dune which blocked the agents' view. They almost collided.

The drivers went into defensive mode and gunned their engines kicking up heavy plumes of powdery sand temporarily blinding the trucker. He slammed on his brakes and nearly tipped over and spilling his multi-million dollar cargo. No one doubted that he was radioing the missile site before they were even out of his sight. They roared north and east in a diagonal across the desert that was completely trackless and devoid of distinguishing features following the *Shamal.*

Ed was on his lap top and inputting GPS coordinates as fast as he could.

He said to Tom Eggerly, "Our best bet is to head to Kuwait. If we can get to highway 95, it'll take us something like four hours to get to the border at Ras al- Khafji. We'll be home safe in Kuwait."

"How many miles is that?" Tom asked as he continued to keep his foot pressing the accelerator to the floor.

"About 282 or 283 miles."

Mac told everyone to drink a lot of water and to try and choke down an MRE. It might be a long while before they would have a chance to refuel.

"Everyone make sure you have at least two loaded firearms. I want all four combat shotguns ready. I think this is going to get close."

He was right.

The three HMMWVs excited a plume of dust larger than a dust-devil whirlwind which could not be missed against the sanitary and formless background of the sand desert. A dozen or more Saudi air force pick-up trucks with 50 caliber machine guns mounted in the truck beds were racing towards the CIA agents and their vehicles. Each pick-up had six men aboard—three in the front and three in the bed. They had been severely threatened by their colonel, and their lives depended on capturing the interlopers for questioning, or, failing that, killing them. In their minds, this was the law of the jungle where the many and the strong prey on the few and the weak. They had no intention in offering their quarries any quarter.

Mac and Ed frantically looked for a place where they could mount a defense, even just high ground. The worst possible scenario was for them to be caught in the open and surrounded.

Mac asked quietly, "Does everyone have a cyanide tablet?"

He looked pointedly at Sybil.

"In my second right lower molar," she said, condemning herself for having allowed her job to put her in such jeopardy and her family possibly being never able to understand why or where she had gone.

Deep breath. There was no time for self-absorption or self-pity. This was fight and flight time, and her adrenaline levels were up. Way up.

"There, behind those rocks. At least they can't get behind us," Ed pointed.

"Okay. Don't settle there before they have to chase around for a while. I think we can take some of them out before they get us."

"*Custer's last*," Sybil thought to herself. "*What an ignominious mess!*"

The Saudis bore closer and closer in on them.

"Start circling. Confuse them. Kill as many trucks as you can. It's more important to get the trucks than the men. We can get away from the men, but not from all of the trucks," Mac ordered.

The lead trucks were now within 100 yards of the CIA HMMWVs and closing fast. Suddenly, the three Hummers did something crazy in the eyes of their pursuers. They turned in wide arcs and came around straight at the pick-up truck cavalry. It made no sense. It was not *halal*. Crazy Americans—at least, they presumed they were Americans. The 50 caliber machine guns in the truck beds were pointed the wrong way. The men in the back frantically worked to re-aim their weapons but found it extremely difficult at the speeds they were traveling and over completely uneven terrain. The first six pick-ups met a furious fusillade from the Americans. Every one of the trucks was put out of commission—some with blown tires, others with dead drivers which resulted in out-of-control crashes; and others were lost because their drivers decided to make a hairpin swerve at the last minute in a deadly game of chicken and lost control.

The Americans disappeared into their own dust and drove away in crazy figure-of-eight patterns. The Saudis could not figure out where they were or what they were doing. They developed a deep sense of having lost their numerical advantage.

The dust encircled the Saudis suggestive of a giant whirlwind. They became confused. Then the Americans came like avenging angels from the rear of the cavalry of pick-up trucks. Another six trucks were put out of commission. It was now rather irrelevant how many Saudis there were. The ones left alive and on the ground were more of a hindrance than a help. Their own trucks began to run the unfortunate stragglers down. No Americans had suffered wounds, and all three HMMWVs were still going strong.

The Hummer driven by Nick Haggerty stopped well behind the fight in a depression that prevented it from being seen by the trucks ahead. The other two HMMWVs came in again from the front like Kamikazes. The pickups tried to scatter. Two stopped and the men in them began to fire wildly at the rapidly zig-zagging Hummers. They were sitting ducks and were annihilated in two passes. Two more pick-ups became litter in the center of the Saudis' advance. The leader now had to admit that things were not going well and called back to base for reinforcements.

The HMMWVs spun around immediately behind the closely grouped attackers and took out three more pickups and a dozen men. There were now fifteen remaining pickups and thirty-five men running about uselessly on the ground. The Americans again did something totally unexpected given the success of their counter-attacking strategy. They turned tail and began to race away.

The Saudis shouted a blood-curdling cheer, "*Allahu-Akbar*!!!"

That was premature. The pickups focused all of their attention on the cowardly fleeing Americans who were trying to scurry away like frightened rabbits. Math was apparently not their strong suit. They lost count and were unaware of Nick Haggerty and his men and their HMMWV which was now advancing from behind them under cover of a dense sand cloud.

Nick had been a soldier and a paramilitary for most of his adult life. He had soldiered with the best.

"*Ayo Gurkhali*!" [The Gurkhas Are Coming], Nick screamed the Gurkha's war cry out the open window and floored the fuel pedal.

They ran over the occasional hapless Saudi airman on the ground and lurched and pirouetted around abandoned trucks. The rearmost three Saudi trucks fell victim to the surprisingly accurate fire from the Americans. Another eight airmen were critically wounded or killed outright. Chaos reigned, and only the Americans seemed to be in command of their own destiny.

Twelve trucks and twenty-seven men remained in the fight on the Saudi side. Their colonel rallied them, and they set off at a pace half again faster than could be managed by the HMMWVs. They began to gain ground, and it was obvious that it was only a matter of time until the arrogant Americans were killed or captured.

The call to base aroused the commanding officer like never before. He called the secret number in Riyadh and was immediately put through to Muhammad al Saud ibn Wahhab. When ibn Wahhab heard the news, he was livid.

"Kill them! Kill them! No, get some to torture you idiot! Bring them to me. They will sing until there is nothing left of them. I will get the F-15s in the air. That will bring this fiasco to an end. You fool. Consider yourself relieved of your command and get into a plane and come to headquarters here in Riyadh as fast as you can make it. Do you understand, you stupid imbecile!?"

Actually, Colonel Ali Mustaffa ibn Abdullah ibn Ghayth was not a fool. He knew in a heartbeat what would happen to him if he showed up in ibn Wahhab's office any time during the rest of his life. So, he got into one of the larger base trucks and made his way to Oman while the confusion still prevailed.

Three F-15E jet fighters—in Saudi hands due to the largesse of the infidel Americans—roared out of the capital city and covered the short distance to the site of the firefight in less than half an hour. There was an impenetrable cover of dust over the area. The pilots surmised from the catastrophic reports coming into headquarters that their forces were in retreat and trying to get to the mountains. That put the Americans in the rear; so, the pilots agreed amongst themselves to strafe the dust column from the rear towards the front—a decision comparable to shooting at a noise on a deer hunt that might be a deer or it might not.

The deadly machine gun, cannon fire, and AIM-9 Sidewinders, AIM-7 Sparrow and AIM-120 AMRAAMs missiles decimated the troops and trucks on the ground. Unfortunately for the Saudis down there in the dust, almost all of the killing occurred as collateral damage. By the time of the next jet fighter pass, there were six pick-up trucks still in motion and 18 live combatants in the trucks. The Saudi stragglers where evidently not fools any more than their commanding officer, and they ran as fast as their physical conditioning would allow in every direction except where the shooting was taking place.

One HMMWV was out of commission and two of the CIA agents were wounded, one critically. Nick Haggerty was hit in the buttocks, a wound which hurt his pride and interfered with his ability to run but was not fatal. He and Leo Conrad did their best to get the badly wounded Chris Stevenson out of harm's way but it was very slow going. It helped that the remaining pick-up trucks were now more or less milling about unsure which way to drive because even their own air force was attacking them. Tom Eggerly and Ed Simonsen decided to make the odds more nearly in their favor before stopping to pick up their wounded.

They roared out of the dust in front of the Saudi trucks and stragglers and had a fast moving turkey shoot. Another eleven Saudis and three of the six still functioning pick-ups were dispatched to Paradise where 77 houris awaited them (presumably). The American Hummers never slowed down or flew in a straight line. They paused to pick up their wounded comrades before streaking towards the previously agreed upon rendezvous point.

The Saudi jet fighters streaked through again laying down a deafening cacophony of automatic weapons fire. None of the Americans were injured on this pass; and fortunately for the Saudi effort, neither were any more of their ground fighters killed or injured. However, the will to fight was waning; and the pace of pursuit slackened significantly.

The three pilots radioed each other questioning the value of further pursuit since they could hardly see a thing on the ground. They admitted that they had no real idea where the Americans were or if they had been so unfortunate as to kill a few of their own people. They squad commander ordered them to return to base.

The Americans parked their vehicles on top of the small mesa they had agreed upon before the fight began. They all rushed to fill the diesel tanks of the two still living HMMWVs and to inspect them for damage.

"Some flesh wounds," Mac quipped, "but nothing in the engine room. We're still good to go."

Ed said, "They're still coming after us. Let's tip one of the vehicles over and set up what we can of a defense. Doc, how about you tend the wounded while we get the guns and ammo ready, okay?"

"Sure," Sybil said.

She was filthy, had a mouth full of dust, and was shaking. She had been shivering earlier when the temperature was only 41°. Now it was just nerves. She steeled her resolve and dragged poor Chris Stevenson as far out of harm's way as she could. She helped Tom Haggerty limp over to a flat rock; so, he could get a little relief from the strain of standing. His gluteal wound had stopped bleeding, indicating that he had not been injured in any major vessel, and he could sort of walk; so, Sybil was sure that he had not had a nerve injury.

She tore open Chris's BDU blouse, and one look told the whole story. He had a centrally placed sucking chest wound. The emergency supplies contained a chest tube and suction apparatus, but the man was so nearly gone that Sybil decided to let him die in peace. She held his head and soothed him until his eyelids came to half closure and his pupils to mid-position and fixed. She closed his eyes and draped a coat over his face. Then she turned to Tom.

"Take off your clothes, please, Tom," she asked.

"I'm not that kind of a boy, Madam," he joked, but laughing was too painful for either of them.

Between them, they got his blood soaked pants off, and Sybil gently turned him onto his side. She washed the wound out with several gallons of their water and powdered it with polysporin antibiotic powder and wound-seal QR powder topped by HemCon Kytostat bandages to stop the remaining bleeding. She wrapped his buttocks and right hip with wide roller gauze and ace wraps and gave him ten milligrams of morphine. He slipped into a drug induced slumber in minutes. His fight was over.

The five defenders were ready for the advancing killers. Sybil made each of them swallow down two bottles of water and eat a Toblerone chocolate bar. They were revived and thanked her. She picked up a combat shot gun and a sniper rifle, her favorite weapons and prepared for battle alongside the other unsung heroes. If this was to be their last day, no one would ever know what happened to them.

No more planes flew over. That was a good sign. There were only three trucks partially filled with fighters coming at them now. They were still 150 yards away, and apparently none of them considered himself enough of a marksman to get out of a truck and try his skill.

That was not the case with Sybil. Her hands and arms were steady as rocks, and her eyes were clear. She kept her forehead free of dripping sweat with a dish towel from the mess kits. She took careful aim, held her breath and exhaled slowly as she squeezed the trigger. There was a very loud report from the end of the fine rifle, and a machine gunner fell off his truck. She fired twice more, hitting one man directly in the chest and missing the third. She was more successful than her killing might have suggested. The truck driver had had enough of trying to be a hero, and he made a sharp right turn and roared away back towards home base. The other two trucks stopped by a small pile of rocks about 50 yards away and worked to make a rude set of breast works as a defensive position.

The distinctive roar of two jet airplanes came roaring towards them. Sybil and her weary comrades-in-arms looked at each other and acknowledged that this was their end. However, Sybil noticed the irregularity first. The planes were coming from the Southeast, not from the direction of the secret base or Riyadh. The next irregularly made the five survivors shout for joy. The jets were F-35 Lightning II stealth fighters, and Saudi Arabia did not have any of them. The CIA agents waggled white undershirts to identify their position. The dust had settled by now, and their flags were obvious. The American pilots stationed in Oman zeroed in on the remaining Saudi rebels cringing behind their useless two foot high rock barricade. Both jets let go an air-to-ground AIM-7 Sparrow rocket, and both missiles were accurate. When the smoke and dust blew away, there was no trace of the two trucks, the six men, or the pile of rocks, just a four feet deep ten feet wide crater. The F-35 pilots waggled their wings at the American CIA agents and arced off back to Oman.

Chapter Ten

KJO Hospital [Al Khafji Joint Operations Hospital], Ras al-Khafji, Saudi-Kuwaiti Neutral Zone, January 13-15, 2016

Agent Tom Haggerty's wound began to fester on the second day of travel across the soft sand. Traction was difficult which made the going slow. Every jouncing bump caused the tough campaigner to groan. Chris Stevenson's body was beginning to ripen despite the layers of covering placed on top of him. They had not seen nor heard any activity on the part of the regular SA armed forces nor from the rebels who were so determined to find and destroy them. The only human activity they saw were tribesmen moving from Saudi Arabia towards Kuwait, Trucial Oman, Muscat, and Oman. As they began to come to the fringes of the Rub al-Khali, the traffic became busier as the nomads freely drove their animals back and forth over the undemarcated borders.

Mac, Ed, and Sybil had a conference that night.

"Look, you guys, Tom is going to get into real trouble if we don't get him to a hospital pronto. He's feverish and sometimes confused. We're not all that far from the KJO Hospital in Ras al-Khafji, which is a pretty up-to-date center. I'm not a big risk taker, but we haven't seen any SA military traffic since we left the vicinity of Al-Ahsa and Dammam. My bet is that they have either decided we are not important, or they just can't find us. I suggest that we get to the highway ASAP and take our chances."

There was a brief discussion, but Tom's progressing condition trumped other concerns. They hid in a small date palm grove through the day then left on a north-east course across the sand towards the junction of Highway 95 and King Fahd Causeway, which connects the Kingdom across the Bay of Bahrain to Bahrain. Two helicopters hovered over them for about half an hour and fired a few desultory rounds in their direction, but the darkness was too deep for them to get a good fix on the two HMMWVs headed for the highway.

"We'll have a couple of hours of cover from darkness once we get to 95; but, after that, we will be visible," Ed said.

"How bad it gets will depend on whether or not we get into significant traffic. I can't see the rebels strafing a bunch of Saudi and international citizens in the hopes that they can take us out, too," Mac said, "but once we see light hitting that highway, we are going to have to fly like a bat and hope to outrun their poor aim. Everybody agree?"

The battle council vote was unanimous, and they plowed through the sand and onto the highway just north of the intersection with the causeway. There was skimpy traffic; so, they put their vehicles into high gear and flew as fast as they could north, incurring the wrath of more sensible drivers. At nine-fifteen a.m. on the morning of the fifteenth, they were

45 miles from the Saudi-Kuwaiti Neutral Zone going almost 90 miles an hour. Their invisibility and luck ran out.

Mac said, "Once we're in the neutral zone, I don't think they will pursue us; so, we are going to go for broke from here on out."

Before he could coax any more speed out of his Hummer, a silver F-15 Eagle swooped out of the sky and strafed the highway in front of them. A cargo truck hauling oil rig equipment was hit and exploded, but they were able to swerve around it and to keep going. The fighter jet made another pass, this time trying to strafe the road and right up their backs. The rounds hit close but were off target by three feet to the left. The shooting stitched a line two miles long parallel to the HMMWVs' path. Several cars and a pick-up truck were hit and stopped, but the Hummers were missed. Ed calculated that they were now in the Neutral Zone, and that they had seen the last effort by the rebels to kill them as they traveled. He couldn't guarantee that they would be safe on the ground, however.

They were nearly out of fuel when they stopped in front of the emergency entrance to the KJO Hospital [Al Khafji Joint Operations Hospital]. Sybil and Mac ran into the ER and rousted up two sleepy orderlies who each brought out a gurney. Sybil followed Tom Haggerty into the treatment area before being ordered out. Mac got a proper body bag for Chris and made sure that he got into the hospital's morgue cooling units so that the rate of decomposition would slow down.

Leo Conrad was a quiet man who never complained or whined. He was intelligent, and all of his suggestions during the mission had been cogent. He had a suggestion now.

"I know this is emotionally difficult, but we are still in considerable danger. Part of our mission is to report what we saw out in that desert and for which we all came close to being killed. Our guys are being taken care of. The docs and nursing staff will get the police and the army in here in short order. That will ensure that our guys stay okay, but it will cost all of us weeks in an unpleasant Saudi prison before it all gets sorted out. We need to move out. We won't be really safe until we get to at least Jaber Al Ali."

Again, there was a consensus, and the team bade Tom goodbye and assured him that the embassy would get people to fetch him back to the States. They joined the throngs on Highway 95, refueled in Jaber Al Ali, and had a necessarily leisurely drive into Kuwait City due to the rush hour commute congestion on the highway.

Private Office of the President of Israel, No. 3 Hanassi Street, Jerusalem, Israel, January 17, 2013, 0835 hrs.
Present: President Levi Menacham Cohen; Prime Minister Barack Har-Segor; Chief of the *Rav Aluf* [General Staff] of the IDF, Lieutenant General Moshe Even-Zahav; Director of Mossad, Elad Ben-Zion.
Re: Mossad report on recent events in Saudi Arabia

"You have the floor and our full attention Elad," President Cohen said gesturing to his most senior intelligence officer.

"Thank you. I will be as brief as possible. We have our American cousins to thank for the information, and the courage and ingenuity of our field agents for the pertinent actions. DCIA Edelweiss called me to let us know that a group of their agents have been poking their noses into some secret Saudi business. It turns out that the business in question was conducted by rebels in the military—air force to be precise—who, as I have suggested before, were planning a nuclear attack on us. We learned specifics: the plan was finalized except for the logistical technicalities. Thermonuclear missile attacks were to take place on December 12 this year, the *Mawlid an-Nabi*—the putative birthdate of The Prophet. Although we have reams of detailed information about the leaders, the location of the bombs, and a great many of the fanatic participants in the program of mass murder, the main fact is that we know the head; and the head has been cut off.

"I did not think that the Wahhabis, and therefore the Saudis permitted celebration of the *Mawlid an-Nabi* in the country," observed Prime Minister Har-Segor.

"True, and even more ironic than that. ibn Wahhab, like all of his kin-folk, is a vociferous opponent of celebrating the Prophets birthdate—calls it *shirq*. Maybe the choice of the day is meant to be ironic or to convey some sort of message. Who can tell with those people?" Gen. Even-Zahav broke in.

"Not I," said the Mossad director. "Our agent—perhaps he could be called the 'Eli Cohen'of our day—has confirmed that Muhammad al Saud ibn Wahhab—the mastermind of the murderous plot—has succumbed to an untimely heart attack. It should not leave this room, but our agent was the cause of that 'heart attack'. Our American cousins—may Jehovah bless their pointy little heads—provided us with an amber-glass stoppered vial of the batrachotoxin of *Phyllobates terribilis*—the beautiful golden poison frog native to the Pacific coast of Colombia that has been used to poison arrow heads by the indigenous hunters for centuries. The toxin is a particularly poisonous steroidal alkaloid secreted from the frog's skin glands. A minute amount of less than 140 micrograms is sufficient to kill a 70 kilogram man. That is about three grains of ordinary table salt. The vial the Amis gave us contained enough poison to kill about 500 men, give or take. One need only place a drop of the colorless, tasteless, viscous liquid in an alcoholic or sweet juice drink or on the tongue of a sleeping person; and the victim will experience almost immediate neuromuscular transmission blockade followed by muscular and respiratory paralysis and a quiet death. Unless the toxin is specifically suspected, the cause of death will be written off as being of natural origin such as a heart attack and further investigation will produce such negative findings that the poison will not be suspected.

"Our Institute agent is a much abused 'hazara' on the wait staff. No one paid him the slightest attention other than to insult him and to inflict blows on him. No one noticed as he went about in his humble way passing out drinks, serving canapés, and bowing obsequiously. And yesterday, no one noticed when he put 20 drops of the batrachotoxin in a hearty, alcohol free, halal approved, Blueberry Cheesecake Ice Cream, an especial favorite of ibn Wahhab. And no one noticed when our agent slipped silently and unobtrusively away. Muhammad al Saud ibn Wahhab died less than two minutes later, and no one suspects us. The unfortunate heart attack victim was buried that very day without an autopsy in strict compliance with Islamic burial rules."

"What does the SA government know about all of this, Elad?" President Cohen asked.

"Nothing about the cause of ibn Wahhab's death and every-thing about the rebel military group that planned the attacks on us—and, more than incidentally—on our esteemed neighbors, the Persians. DCIA Edelweiss and I chatted this morning. A group of American CIA agents, whom he would not name, visited the Eastern Province and gathered some startling news which was quickly transmitted to Langley and on to the president. President Willets and DCIA Edelweiss contacted their counterparts, King Khulus and Abu Bakr

Wasem. Our contacts tell us that a cleansing operation is going into motion as we speak. Our American and Saudi friends have asked us to keep this a secret among us. We have been only too happy to oblige."

"Incredibly fine work, Elad. I think there ought to be a citation for your agent. Someday, the nation should know who he or she is."

"Thank you, Mr. President. We will confer the honor and will let the agent know of your gratitude."

Chapter Eleven

**SANG [Saudi Arabian National Guard] Headquarters],
KAAB [King Abdulaziz Mechanized Brigade], Hofuf,
Saudi Arabia, January 17, 2016, 1000 hrs, CUT
[Coordinated Universal Time].**

The National Guard [Arabic: *al-ḥaras al-Waṭani* or White Army]—25,000 tribal militia troops—assembled at the double on the parade grounds in full battle dress and stood at rapt attention. Prince Aban Shadid Al Sharifi ibn Saud—second in command in the ministry and the on-site commander of all Eastern National Guard troops—tapped on his microphone to gain the attention of his men. He held his revered position because of his close identification with the tribal leaders who supplied the men who were fanatically loyal protectors of the Saud family.

"Today, we shall face a band of traitors to our army, our nation, the Saud family, and our God. I want every man to fight like a lion, to face death with courage, and to wipe out this pestilence. Allah is with you!"

As if one man, the militia responded with a *"Allahu Akbar*!!!" which could be heard five miles away across the gently sifting sand of the desert stretching off to the south.

The superbly disciplined SANG troops of the KAAB [King Abdulaziz Mechanized Brigade] recruited from Saudi tribes mounted up on their armored fighting vehicles and armored personnel carriers. Overhead, they were supported by the brigade's own helicopters and light aircraft. 20,000 feet above them, regular army MIGs and F-15 silver Eagle killer jets circled, waiting like great vultures. On the ground, light tanks, artillery caissons, and towed 155 mm M-198 howitzers began to move inexorably south with the troops. The troops were proud and very highly trained. They wore the traditional red-checkered keffiyeh Arab headdress and thawbs with crossed bandoliers. It was a stirring and formidable sight.

In the secret desert missile site and nuclear storage facility, Lt. Col. Ibrahim Nassar ibn Abdul Muhaymin—named acting commanding officer after the desertion of Col. Ishmail Khuzaymah to Oman—took a deep breath and put in a call to Riyadh to the secret mission headquarters. He was very mindful of the wrath expended against his predecessor and was not altogether fond of the idea that his name would be associated with this upcoming battle. Unlike headquarters, he had no illusions of victory for his small force.

"Greetings from the friends of Allah, SWT [*Subhana Wa Tala*—ALLAH, The Sacred and The Mighty]. What is needed?"

"This is Col. Nassar. I need to receive orders from our fearless leader, Muhammad al Saud ibn Wahhab."

"He is…not available. Proceed with 'Final Day's Order, 2016-01-SAA'."

The Lt. Col. was not sure what to make of that message. Ibn Wahhab was always available to his field commanders, especially when the call came via the red phone. He was on his own.

The scouts reported that the SANG militia was now in motion, and their intent could not be misconstrued. He walked into the computer control room and summoned the Senior Master Sergeant.

"Follow me. Bring your key."

The two somber men walked to a dual set of control panels.

"On my count of three, insert your key."

Both men inserted their keys into the slots on their respective panels.

"On my count of two, turn your key to the right."

"One...two."

Within a second of the turn of those keys, the silos opened and three large DF-3 [Chinese Dongfeng-3] middle-range missiles, armed with their new nuclear warheads, rose up to the top of their silos.

"Press the 'fire' button, Senior Master Sergeant. Do it now."

The two men pressed firmly on their two-inch wide domed red buttons, and missiles targeting Tel Aviv, Jerusalem, and Tehran escaped the silos in a deafening blast.

-**White House War Room, January 16, 2016, 1300 hrs CUT [Coordinated Universal Time].**
-**Present: POTUS; DCIA; JCS, CIA Special Agent, Sybil Norcroft; CIA Special Agent Mac Young.**
-**War Room Niavaran Palace, Northern Tehran, Islamic Republic of Iran, January 16, 2016, 1330 hrs CUT**
Present: Supreme Leader the Grand Ayatollah, Ali ibn Muhammad Norouzi; Hosseini Jahanbani, Chief of

Staff; Saeed Abdullahi, President of the Republic of Iran; Pirooz ibn Rahmani, Chief of Staff of the Armed Forces of the Republic of Iran; Kourosh Kashani, Head of AEOI [the Atomic Energy Organization of Iran]; Mullah, Ali Moqtada Tabatabaei, Director of MOIS [the Ministry of Intelligence and Security]; and Hamid Yousefi, Director of MISIRI—VEVAK [the Ministry of Intelligence and National Security of the Islamic Republic of Iran].

-Ephraim Brigade Base temporary War Room near Kedumim, Jerusalem 1200 hrs CUT

Present: President Levi Menacham Cohen; Prime Minister Barack Har-Segor; Chief of the *Rav Aluf* [General Staff] of the IDF; Lieutenant General Moshe Even-Zahav; Director of Mossad, Elad Ben-Zion.

The mood in each of the rooms was electric with anticipation of ultimate doom or victory. The next few seconds would decide which. Israel had the most to lose and had made the fateful decision to trust the Americans that their cyber wizardry would save the day.

The high definition satellite video was centered on an obscure and heretofore entirely secret missile installation located in the *Rub' al Khali* desert close to the northern border of Yemen. Fortunately for the observers, it was a clear day, unlike the recent spate of *shamals* that plagued the area in the past two weeks. The computers in each war room were synchronized with those of the missile base thanks to the CIA, VEVAK, and Mossad spies who had independently hacked the sensitive Saudi secret headquarters computers in Riyadh.

The countdown in each room began: ten, niner, eight, seven, six, fiver, four, three, two, one.

The satellite feed screens lit up with three almost simultaneous explosions. In each of the three rooms, someone asked the inevitable question: were those nuclear explosions?

And, in each room, a technologist replied: no, those were nothing more than three TNT explosions in the middle of the Saudi Arabian desert.

There was a pause then shouts for joy, high fives, making signs of the cross, kissing stars of David, and fingering prayer beads. Then the people who had been sitting on the edges of their chairs afraid that they were about to witness the beginning of Armageddon, slumped into an almost dazed relief.

Agent Norcroft broke the silence in the White House War Room, "What just happened? I saw explosions, and you are saying that they were not from nuclear bombs."

DCIA Edelweiss said to everyone, "Not nucs. The explosions were the igniter TNT which exploded out of synch with the nuclear material and at the wrong time and in the wrong place. Dr. Norcroft, the USB flash drive you inserted into in the Al-Ahsa missile base computers took over the bombing instructions. The missiles squirted out of their silos then took a nose-dive and that set off their TNT. The HEU in the bombs has to have a very precise timing in order to be ignited, and in this case that was—in highly technical terms—'screwed-up royally'. Congratulations Agent. All of the sacrifices of you and your men saved the day and the Middle-East for yet another day in this seemingly unending religious war of attrition."

Sybil blinked back a tear. She was not the only one in those three powerful rooms who did.

Covert Saudi Nuclear Storage and Missile Facility Somewhere in the *Rub' al Khali,* Near the Northern Border with Yemen, January 16, 2016, 1024 hrs. CUT

Immediately after pushing the 'fire' buttons, Lt. Col. Nassar issued his orders over the base intercom system: "Let every man fight to the death against the incoming infidels!"

Every battle station was manned, and every weapon readied, including surface-to-surface missiles. No one flinched at the idea that he would shortly be killing his own people, his comrades-in-arms of a scant few days previously.

Outside, the tribal militia moved into the area with force. Prince Aban Shadid Al Sharifi ibn Saud issued his orders: "Take as many as possible alive. We need to obtain intelligence about this illegal and wicked operation. Now, go and do your duty with discipline. I have complete faith in you, my brethren."

Inside the silo, Lt. Col. Nassar realized with horror that his nuclear missiles had malfunctioned. Instead of the glorious news that Tehran, Tel Aviv, and Jerusalem had been turned into unlivable radioactive craters, his own fortress had been irretrievably ruined. All hope was lost. He and his men vowed to fight to the last man and to die as martyrs. There was no other viable option.

Once the tribal militia gathered in force surrounding the silo and nuclear weapon storage facilities, their commander, Prince Aban Shadid Al Sharifi ibn Saud, called out to the defenders over the sophisticated sound system that he insisted be brought to the battle front.

"Colonel Nassar and all men in the compound. In five minutes, you will march out of your facility empty-handed with your hands high above your heads. You must hurry now to stack all weapons in the middle of your second floor lobby.

If you surrender with honor, your lives will be spared. The lives of your parents, your lives, and your children will be spared. Failure to do that will result in an attack the likes of which you have never known. Survivors will be beheaded. Wives, children, old parents, grandparents, cousins out to the 6th degree will be hunted down and sold into slavery. Girls and young women will become the sexual slaves of my brave tribal militiamen. They do not take kindly to traitors to the Saud family. You need not make a verbal reply. You actions will speak for themselves."

A signal officer was assigned to count down every thirty second interval. When the count was down to one minute, a barrage of bullets, grenades, LAWs rockets, and flame throwers came roaring out of the buildings. The militiamen were out of range for most of the ordinance; and only three were wounded, none seriously; and no one was killed.

Prince ibn Saud ordered his executive officer to lead the troops and to do what was necessary, but to be certain that as many senior officers and enlisted men as possible were captured alive.

Col. Sheikh Mustafa ibn Muhammad al-Achmed, waved his index finger in a circular motion high above his head then pointed in the direction of the silo. Like a robot army, the troop trucks and armed personnel carriers started forward. Artillery barrels lowered into an aiming position that was targeted to wipe out the first and second floors. The cannons remained silent, however. Instead of meeting increased fire from the silo and other buildings, the fusillade diminished as the militia moved inexorably forward.

PSYOP teams began to broad cast at an ear rupturing volume Wagner's, *the Cry of the Valkyries*, which is a disturbing piece of dark music. Then, the sound system blared out *El Degüello*, a song that appealed to the enemy to surrender or die by the sword. It was played by General Santa Anna who wanted to frighten the defenders of the Alamo into either fleeing or surrendering. It signified that no quarter would be given. The literal translation of the song title is "slit-throat". Then, there was a five minute period of silence. It was so disconcerting and eerie, that even the defenders ceased firing. Finally, a clear but piercing rendition was played of the universally recognized bugle call, *Taps*. The implication was obvious.

Al-Achmed called out through the amplified megaphone system, "Commence firing."

The sky was filled with fire and bullet tracers. The ground rumbled and shook. The buildings began to crumble, and men began to scream in fear and pain and for mercy that would not come.

The battle was over in five minutes. As soon as the first few survivors, most wounded and many beyond help, appeared outside the buildings, Col. al Achmed ordered a cease fire. The tribal militiamen swarmed around the helpless and defeated airmen and divested them of their weapons and their dignity. Every man was stripped naked and placed in plastic restraints. They were linked to each other with dog collars and tough chains. In all, 121 men staggered out to be loaded into troop trucks. They were almost stacked on top of each other. Pleas for help with bleeding wounds, dangling limbs, blind eyes, extravasating vessels, herniating guts, and desperate thirst went unheeded.

The executive officer's body was found with a suicide bullet hole in his right temple. After a brief search, Lt. Col. Nassar was found in a feeble disguise. He had taken the clothes off a dead private. Unfortunately, for him, the entire uniform was more than a size too small, and his limp in the small blistering boots made him stand out like a clown walker. He was given a special ride with Prince ibn Saud back to headquarters in Hofuf. The ride was the least unpleasant experience of his day, and for the next three months he was kept alive. He did turn out to be a veritable fount of information. By the end of February, 2,014 officers and men were arrested before the regular army and SANG were satisfied that the traitors were all identified. All 2,014 were beheaded on the bases from which they had defected to become part of Muhammad al Saud ibn Wahhab's overly ambitious terrorist plot.

In an act unprecedented in geopolitics, King Khulus Shafique ibn Nawwaf bin Abdulaziz formally apologized to the President of Israel and the Supreme Leader of the Islamic Republic of Iran for the acts of a few Saudis who had disgraced the nation. In what had to be an overwhelmingly painful act of loss of face, the king apologized on behalf of Saudi Arabia and the 15,000 members of the Saud family. The president and the Supreme Leader returned terse 'thank-you' notes through their respective foreign ministers.

92

Chapter Twelve

Wisconsin Avenue, NW, Georgetown, Washington D.C., January 18, 2015, 1900 hrs.

"Okay!" Charles said, "it was a great dinner and it is great to have all of us back together in our own home at the same time. That's becoming something of an unusual combination of schedules of late."

"I'm sorry," Sybil said, "but I have pretty good news. I no longer have to get to work every day, and I won't have to travel for Wolf News ever again. I was thinking of running for PTA president and taking up quilting at home."

She said it perfectly drily, and in ten seconds all three of them were laughing so hard that tears were streaming down their cheeks.

"Huh!" Sybil said in mock offense at the suggestion that she was being disingenuous.

"Good to hear," both Cerisse and her father chorused; and again the three had a laugh.

"I really have straightened up most of my overseas business and should be home almost all of the time for the next four months," Charles said. "Seems like another car trip or a stay-at-home-and-enjoy-our-town vacation would be in order."

Cerisse took immediate advantage, "Let's go to Hawaii. I have heard such great stuff about it. Maybe it could be my senior trip before I leave home for college."

That came as a jolt. Not unexpected, since Cerisse was nearing the end of her schooling in Georgetown Visitation Preparatory School. She had grown up so fast, Sybil thought. The show tune, *Sunrise, Sunset*, from *Fiddler on the Roof* intruded from somewhere in her subconscious:

"Is this the little girl I carried,
Is this the little boy at play?
I don't remember growing older,
When did they?
When did she get to be a beauty,
When did he grow to be so tall?
Wasn't it yesterday when they were small?
Sunrise, sunset, sunrise, sunset
Swiftly flow the days..."

She was unaware that she was humming, and that she had sung very quietly the line, "Wasn't it yesterday when she was small..." Charles looked at her and smiled—great minds...

"Report time," Charles said, taking his role as the pater familias. "Cerisse, you go first. We haven't given each other a good report for more than a couple of weeks."

"Not much to tell," she said, which was her usual introductory sentence before launching into a three volume introduction to the history of the world.

Her parents raised their eyebrows.

She laughed her infectious self-deprecating laugh and knew that she had their rapt attention.

"Well…" she drew out the word, "there are a couple of things…"

"Out with it," Charles said.

"Well…for one thing, I have a new boyfriend."

Both parents emitted a theatrical audible groan.

"This one doesn't sell drugs, isn't in a gang; and he doesn't have any tattoos anywhere."

Both parents raised their eyebrows, and it was not theatrical.

"Hey, at least I don't think he does…he's not the type," Cerisse said and probably blushed, but no one would have been able tell, "jeez."

"Okay," Sybil laughed, "Go on."

"I hope you like him. He's a little stiff and too certain about what he wants to do; and, uh that he wants me to hitch my wagon to his star, I think is the way he put it."

"He's driven, you say," Charles observed.

"Let me guess," Sybil said and paused, "he's going to be a pre-med student, and he is absolutely certain that he is going to be a doctor. Am I close?"

"Right on," Cerisse said and gave her mother a big affectionate smile.

Sybil returned the smile with all of its sincerity and worked not to show her relief.

"Okay, tell us about him," Charles said.

"Accepted to Howard, is an Episcopalian, plays water polo, likes kids and dogs; and…he loves me."

Even the whites of her eyes blushed.

Both parents held her in a sandwich embrace. The news was everything they had hoped for.

"Are you planning to apply to Howard, Cerisse?" Sybil asked.

Cerisse laughed, "Already did. I got accepted. I waited until today to share all of this stuff with you when you were both home."

"Let me guess," Charles said, "pre-med?"

"Nope."

"Nope?!"

"Pre-neurosurgery."

They all laughed uproariously as if there were such an undergraduate program as 'pre-neurosurgery'; but Sybil knew that all prospective neurosurgeons were driven; and that was how they got into residency programs.

"Really...neurosurgery?"

"I grew up after I learned about Andy Witcomb. Mama, you are my role model. I really do want to be a neurosurgeon. I plan to work really hard."

"The both of you have a thought disorder," Charles said with a warm harrumph.

"Okay," Cerisse said, "it's your turn, Mama."

"Not much to tell. I traveled around giving speeches to show that the Surgeon General of the United States knows a little something about medical problems and to do some pol-iticking for the president. It was pretty interesting in Saudi Arabia, I have to admit. You would not believe what they have accomplished in the desert."

Charles looked at his wife to see if he could discern any dissembling, but he decided that she was much too good of a poker player to give herself away. He thought it was probably a pretty useful trait for a woman in her line of work—her new line of work.

"Your turn, Charles."

"Well, nothing that would interest the younger set; but I did have a good time in Europe and clinched what is likely to be the deal of my life. European Consolidated Foods—the largest agri-business outside of the United States—has agreed to merge with Argos Daniels Mitzuki Global Company. The new company is going to be called, Amereurope Consolidated Agricultural Products. We will buy out their executive staff; they will turn over all of their assets and will share profits from future business on a 40-60% basis."

"And, the new CEO?" Sybil asked.

"*Moi.*"

"Great, Daddy, now you will get to work on your French pronunciation," Cerisse said; she was native-fluent in the language and was the only one who could get away with a critique of her father's French language proficiency.

Sybil had to be de-briefed by the DCIA before she could get away with her family; that took two full days. As a courtesy, she informed the president that she would be out west for two weeks and that her assistant would be minding the Surgeon General's shop. He was a better manager than she was anyway. President Willets thanked her profusely once again for her service in Saudi Arabia and told her again that he was sorry that so much of what she had to do was secret, and she could probably never be able to share it outside the very few with a need to know. He genuinely regretted that she could not get the credit due her, but that was the way things were. She smiled and thanked him for his concern.

"*Quite a woman,*" the president mused, "*she's a pistol and more than that, a superb decision maker.*"

He made another tick in his mental notebook about Sybil Norcroft.

Goblin Valley State Park Camp Ground, Southeastern Utah, January 29, 2016

It was brisk, not actually cold in the park. Cerisse was charmed by seeing her own breath. Her experience with cold was so limited from her life in the Congo, that she had never seen that phenomenon before. The Danielses were in their second day camping there, and Cerisse had not yet tired of running around playing hide-and-seek among the goblins and hoo-doos. Goblin Valley is almost unique among state and national parks in the U.S. It is an incredible insight into geological history. Surrounding the small valley full of bright red sandstone goblins are exposed cliffs with parallel layers of rock bared by eons of erosion. The origin of the goblins came about because of the uneven hardness of sandstone, with some patches resisting the processes of erosion better than others. When the softer material is removed by wind and water, there are left thousands of strange, fascinating, and unique, geologic goblins. Because the tops of the goblin formations are larger than their 'stems', the formations were referred to by early explorers as mushrooms.

Sybil had been there with a school group during her junior high years and remembered how much fun it was to cavort around in the incredible structures. All of the tensions of her CIA involvement during the last several weeks fell away as she played like a child. Cerisse had boundless energy and worked hard at exhausting her willing but inadequate parents.

They camped two days each in Dead Horse, Green River, Coral Pink Sand Dunes, and Kodachrome Basin State Parks, and all of them were thrilled and excited by the radiant colors and the great hiking trails. As they went, Charles taught Cerisse and Sybil about the early Anasazi Indian people, the mountain men—tractors and trailers, Cerisse called them—

and the "polygs"—Mormon polygamists who once hid out among the twisted, seemingly endless valleys and ravines from the Federals who came after them to arrest them for practicing an unpopular form of marriage and for their different religious beliefs. The U.S. government finally abandoned its hunt because it was too expensive, too time consuming, and most of the hunters did not believe in the mission anyway.

The family spent the last two days in a whirl-wind tour of the magnificent national parks in the colorful state: Arches, Bryce, Canyonlands, Capitol Reef, and Zion. They all realized that they did not have enough time to give those marvelous places an adequate visit let alone to hike into the Grand Canyon, see the falls of the Havasupi, Mesa Verde, Lake Powell, Horseshoe Bend, Santa Fe, and on and on, of the Grand Circle of portions of five states—Arizona, New Mexico, Colorado, Utah and Nevada.

"Daddy, I don't see why anyone wants to go to a city. They're all alike, but these places are part of heaven. Thank you so much for taking us. We have to come again. Promise!"

"I promise, love."

Chapter Thirteen

DHCPP [Division of High-Consequence Pathogens and Pathology], Office of the Director, CDC [Centers for Disease Control and Prevention], 1600 Clifton Rd. Atlanta, Georgia, February 16, 2016, 0900 hrs
VSPB [Viral Special Pathogens Branch], Emergency Session
Present: DCDC, DVSPB, Surgeon General, SHHS, DIDPB, DOHIV/AIDS & IDP

The director of the VSPB, Rachel Martin, Ph.D., had taken the lead to organize the emergency session of the nation's ranking governmental health officers. Every individual present on that frigid February morning was extremely busy and responsible for major elements of the health care system; so, when they got the call, it was apparent that a serious problem was present or in the offing.

Dr. Martin greeted the assembled officials and launched into the reason for calling them together, "As you all know, our day-to-day work involves the investigation of weird viruses—usually those terrifying monsters that cause hemorrhagic fevers with such a high fatality rate. Dr. Norcroft knows up close and personal about Marburg virus and the terrible epidemic caused by weaponization of that pathogen. So we here at the VSPB are familiar with Ebola, Marburg, Lassa fever, Rift Valley fever, Crimean-Congo hemorrhagic fever, Arena, and Hanta virus species, and some additional recently identified and emerging viral species.

"All of those put together have not killed as many people of the earth as the so-called 'Spanish' influenza virus which caused the pandemic of 1918–1919. That one virus with its extraordinarily virulent strain caused more than 50 million deaths worldwide. To put that into perspective, more people lost their lives from the H_5N_1 virus than from all other causes of World War I put together. Not even the Great Plague of the 1300s killed as many people although it set back civilization by 100 or more years. We have had occasional scares over the decades since; but, with quick and concerted effort, we have so far managed to avoid a major pandemic.

"So far..."

She let the sentence with its implications dangle for a pregnant moment.

"But...we have a report from Hong Kong of three large chicken farms that are finding dead chickens which test positive for H_5N_1 and a pig farm in Portugal with several sick pigs which also test positive. Dr. Norcroft will be unhappy to learn that the pig farm is immediately adjacent to a huge chicken ranch—100s of thousands of chickens shipped every month—owned by Charles Daniels—Sybil's husband—Amereurope Consolidated Agricultural Products. The worst thing is that in Hong Kong and Beijing there are four verified cases in humans, and in Portugal, there have been eleven. Three of those have died. So, Dr. Margoles, Secretary of

Health and Human Services, has asked that we at the VSPB collect, preserve, and protect all samples of the virus. We have the capability on site and can collect everything that fits into the category of BSL-4 [Biosafety Level 4] pathogens. The IDPB [Infectious Disease Pathology Branch] at the CDC will assist VSPB with diagnostic pathology and surveillance. Because the threat is so serious, the OHIV/AIDS & IDP [Office of HIV/AIDS and Infectious Disease Policy] will take charge of identifying and tracking case occurrence.

Sybil entered the presentation, "That leaves the clinical diagnosing and treating of disease victims, managing quarantine, disseminating educational information, and conveying instructions and even orders from the federal and state governments to our citizens. Then, there will be the issues tangled up with international cooperation."

Secretary Frank Margoles of the HHS Department added, "Which includes the massive costs of exterminating millions of meat animals and destroying businesses and livelihoods."

Donovan Michael Cartwright, the DOHIV/AIDS & IDP started to say, "Maybe we're being a bit…" when Dr. Martin received a fire-alarm tone on her i-Pad.

"Pardon me, I have to get this," she said.

Two minutes later, her face visibly paled, and she looked up and announced, "Pardon me, Dr. Cartwright, but we are not even a bit premature. Our agents in Spain, Italy, and Portugal report five hundred new cases of H_5N_1 in the last 24 hours, and reports from the PRC [Peoples Republic of China] and the ROC [Republic of China—Taiwan] show upwards of a 1000 cases and more coming in all the time. All of these sites receive large shipments of chickens and/or pork from the primary animal host sites, and they all have brisk international travel, including to the United States. We have already initiated a re-evaluation of the H_5N_1 virus genome from the latest cases. If, as I suspect, there has been a viable mutation in the virus, we may be on our way to seeing the mother of all pandemics. Let me remind you of the massive influx of airline passengers into this country from Asia and Europe every day."

"How are we doing on getting out this year's flu vaccine?" Sybil asked.

"Not quite ready," Dr. Cartwright said, "but that may not even be relevant. If, as I postulated, there has been a genome mutational change, it is more likely than not that this year's vaccine will be impotent against the new killer."

A very sobered Sybil suggested to Dr. Cartwright, "It seems prudent for each of us here in this room to get into motion. Maybe we should all get our assignments before we are so behind that we become irrelevant."

"I agree, Gen. Norcroft. All right, IDPB, the VSPB, and the OHIV/AIDS & IDP have their work cut out. Because the threat is so serious, I will commit the HHS Department to be responsible for notifying the states' HHS departments and to begin the collection of treatment facilities and equipment for the management of quarantined patients. We will also communicate with the president and the cabinet to put a mass inoculation and quarantine program into effect even if we don't need it in the end. National Influenza Vaccination Week is coming up in two weeks. Maybe we can aim for a nationwide project for that week."

Sybil thought grimly, *"And about that time, pigs will fly. We don't even have pharmaceutical companies lined up with the capability to determine what vaccine to make, how to produce it in mass quantities, and how and where to administer it."*

Her iPhone vibrated.

She said "hello" softly to it, then listened. She, too, turned pale.

"Sybil," she heard the distraught voice of her husband say, "we are ruined in Europe. Our chicken and pig farms in Spain, Portugal, and Italy are full of some new virus—maybe the one that caused the 1918 pandemic. We have to destroy every last animal. I am grief stricken for our employees; there will be a huge recession in Europe; and even if we can survive what has happened, it will take years for us to be able to rehire any significant number of employees. And that doesn't even include the horrific human costs; we know of at least thirty deaths so far. This flu seems to be some kind of super-fast, super-virulent strain. We are rushing to put up emergency treatment tents on the property, but it looks like we're too little and too late. I only hope this thing is contained to Europe."

"Too late, Charles. It is looks like it is going through Asia like a hurricane. No confirmed cases in the U.S. so far, but I am not hopeful. I am in Atlanta attending an emergency meeting. Look, get yourself and Cerisse a flu shot right now. I am going to call in prescriptions for Cipro for you. Start them today. The world is going to run out of drugs in a matter of days—if not hours—once this hits the news."

"Everything okay, Dr. Norcroft?" the HHS Secretary asked solicitously.

"No. More bad news from Europe. What do you want the Surgeon General's office to do?"

"First—and this morning—get hold of your media contacts and get out a sensible, not-time-to-panic message for radio, TV, internet, social media, and print media. Please take charge of informing the heads of all of the major medical organizations and have them pass the information on to their members and the members on to the hospitals and their patients. We have to get in front of this."

"Who should inform the big pharma companies?" Sybil asked Secretary Morales.

"We are all swamped. I understand you are tough, Sybil; and that's what we are going to need. Big pharma will dig in their heels unless they get money up front. In my experience, all they relate to is their bottom line. And, they will probably be scared to death at the prospects of thousands of law suits if everything doesn't turn out just right. Prepare a letter guaranteeing them immunity and twist their arms into doing the research and getting us a new vaccine as fast as humanly possible. You can work with our Jeanine Franklin, head of CDC's Influenza Division. She heads up our collaboration center—one of five WHO Centers—which receives and tests thousands of influenza viruses from around the world each year and collaborates with other WHO Centers and National Influenza Centers around the world in the yearly seasonal vaccine virus selection process for the Southern and Northern Hemispheres. This catches us with our metaphorical pants down. She will welcome the help. The two of you should get going today to get the committee into motion and to get big pharma to do their patriotic bit."

"I'll contact her today."

By the time Sybil called in her family's promised prescriptions and made an appointment of meet with Dr. Franklin on the sixth floor of the same building in which she was sitting, Sybil was bombarded with more bad news. Every time she tapped her Safari app to check on internet information and her own iPhone address book, she was stunned over again with the degree of escalation of the disease. By noon, cases were being reported in Los Angeles, Seattle, Salt Lake City,

Omaha, Charlottesville, Pittsburgh, and New York City. It was no longer an Asian and European problem.

A week later, the scientists at the IDPB [Infectious Disease Pathology Branch] had been able to sequence the entire genome of the new virus. There were two mutations, both viable, which apparently gave the dangerous virus its virulence. They were investigating a human case in Des Moines that might have a third mutation which would indicate that the virus was evolving at an unprecedented rate. That was a cause for fear—perhaps the virus was beyond control and no vaccine could be developed that would meet the changes it was undergoing. But, it was also possible, the scientists told Sybil, that the virus could evolve lethal mutations and burn itself out. It was at least a small ray of hope.

Chapter Fourteen

Buy-Rite Pharmaceutical Corporation Headquarters, Erastus Corning Tower, Capitol Hill, Albany, New York, February 18, 2016, 1000 hrs

Sybil selected Buy-Rite Pharmaceuticals—the world's largest manufacturer and distributor of prescription pharmaceuticals—because of its size and influence, but also because the CEO Cramer Montgomery and her husband, Charles Daniels, were friends from their undergraduate days in Amherst College. The international corporation had an entire division dedicated to R&D and marketing of vaccines. They made billions of dollars in profits every year from the sales of their influenza vaccines.

"Hello, Sybil," the portly CEO said and gave her a straight shoulder embrace and a brush-by kiss on the cheek as he ushered her into his office. "Congratulations are over-due for your appointment as the Surgeon General. I'm flattered to have you visit our place."

"Thanks, I'm glad to be here and that you were so obliging on short notice."

"That's what friends are for. Speaking of friends, how is Charles getting along? Kind of a tough row to hoe this past week, I gather?"

"That's true and not unique to him. I'm sure you are keeping up with the growing pandemic. That's why I'm here."

"Hmmh, my dear, calling it a pandemic may be a bit of hyperbole at this point. Our experts think it will likely blow over in a month or so, and we will be able to get back to business as usual and make a vaccine for the regular flu season."

"Cramer, everything our research tells us, and certainly my gut feeling is that this is far more than a passing blip on the screen of epidemics over the course of history. Even if it doesn't amount to much, we are going to need a new vaccine for a new and more virulent flu this go around, and it has got to get out in record time."

"What is it about this virus that has got you so worked up, Madam Surgeon General. Remember back in…what was it? '05? When we had this same scare from bird flu? That didn't amount of a hill of beans."

"This H_5N_1 virus has mutated—evolved—into a highly contagious, rapidly spreading, lethal new entity. The genome is different and evolving as we sit here. We must stop its progress while we can."

"You know, Sybil, you'd be better off to back away from that talk about evolution and genomes. People don't like it, and you will get branded as one of those anti-Bible science nuts if you aren't careful. Bad for marketing, and not the kind of atheistic philosophy you want to instill in your kids, right? I mean, I read a transcript of your testimony before the

Senate nomination hearing. You about lost the nomination over talk like that."

Sybil was seething and had to choke down the bile. She needed to get this man and his company working for the good of the people. He was obviously testing out the arguments he would use as he marketed against the government's new initiative which did not fit his business model.

"We need a vaccine, Cramer. We need your help. I was hoping you might help lobby your fellow CEOs to get the project underway."

"Even if we didn't have other opinions about the need for a new vaccine, there are questions of payment, indemnification, and help taking the onus away from us if there are problems with a new and largely untried vaccine. Do you have answers for that?"

"I do. I can get you indemnity—immunity. You can make huge profits and all kinds of good will from your spending public. That's all good marketing, right, Cramer?"

She had to fight down the urge to roll her eyes or to wretch.

"About prices. Is that pinko Willets going to put an anti-gouging clause in the deal he comes up with?"

"I can't answer that, but the president needs this; and the people need this. It probably would be a good idea not to press your luck too far. Here is exactly what I want. Day after tomorrow, you and I and your friends in the vaccine making business have a conference call. I did not like the deal that President Obama made with the insurance companies, and I won't like the deal I broker for the vaccine. But I'll live with it. I suggest you do the same."

"I'll set it up, since you put it so nicely, Sybil. Looks like you're learning…starting to run with the big dogs."

"Thanks for your time, Cramer. I'll show myself out."

County/USC [Los Angeles County Hospital]—condemned and abandoned in 2003 as a fire and earthquake hazard—1983 Marengo Street, Los Angeles, California, March 1, 2016

The largest public hospital in the country was abandoned as unsafe and inappropriate, even racist, for its clientele—the black and brown people of the county—13 years ago. Suitable hospitals were designated in the Valley, but poor people could not afford the bus fare to get to them. Now, no one had a choice. The 600 bed facility had to undergo a massive renovation to make even safe to bring patients in. There were plenty of patients. The 600 beds became 858 with more than 150 people lining the hallways. The quarantine applied to the hospital, not to any particular patient. Anyone with the flu was taken there. Other public and private hospitals rebelled at having to admit people with influenza for good reason. Wherever a person with the flu stayed, death and contagion followed. Every effort was taken to give good care, but there were too many people and too few caregivers. The doctors, nurses, and orderlies shuffled around exhausted in their hazmat suits. Children were terrified of the alien figures that attended them. Their parents were too sick to help.

The position of quarantine officer in chief had devolved to Sybil Norcroft, M.D., Ph.D., F.A.C.S., Surgeon General of the United States. She was also the government officer responsible for dealing with the myriad details and problems of getting a vaccine into production. The logistics involved bordered on the impossible. The CDC and its divisions had found four different mutant viruses that remained virulent and made the development of a single vaccine highly problematical. So, the CDC began to attack the problem of how the virus functioned in much the same way as they had the

HIV pathogen. Some progress was being made; the result would be a drug, not a vaccine; and it would not be available for clinical use any time soon.

The huge and uninviting county hospital was only one of 14 Sybil had worked with local medical and hospital societies to bring into a functional state. In the fourteen days since the discovery was made that a new H_5N_1 virus was on the scene, 183,482 cases of influenza had been diagnosed in the United States; 22,598 people had died—mostly the very young and the very old—but the mid-range age group was beginning to catch up. Mortuaries were becoming unable to keep up. In areas of rural China, the PRC was resorting to mass burials because the mortuary services of the country were failing. In Fort Riley, Kansas—home of the Big Red One—a barracks full of men and women going through boot camp registered two cases on the second day of the pandemic, and on the day Sybil visited County USC, all of those previously very healthy young people were dead.

Sybil made somber rounds and talked to patients and staff throughout the venerable old hospital. She had nothing to offer except sympathy. The nation's supply of Cipro and anti-virals was exhausted and none would be available for month. There was no vaccine. There was a mood approaching despair in the country. There was also anger.

Using social media, a group of Tea Party activists blamed the president and his health care appointees for the disease, its path of death and maiming, and the failure to produce a vaccine, or to reign in the greedy big pharma companies. They were making real headway to gather sufficient signatures to hold recall elections and impeachment procedures. Sybil was one of those named—a far cry from her stellar ratings of only a few months previously. When she got back to her Washington office, a Congressional subpoena was waiting for her.

That evening, she came home in a deep funk. Charles and Cerisse had been following the news and were at a loss for words to cheer her up other than to tell her that they loved her and respected her for what she was trying to do. Cerisse made an interesting observation.

"Mama, I have been watching the people wherever I go. The little kids and the old people are a lot fewer than they used to be. But teenagers like me don't seem to have been hit so hard. In fact, I don't think any of my friends have been sick, and I don't know of a single teenager who has died. Why do you think there is that difference?"

"Beats me, Cerisse, but you may be on to something. I am going to get the CDC to look into it. Maybe we can come up with something that will help."

The Congressional hearing was devastating. Sybil was charged with everything from malfeasance in office, theft of government funds, having special privileges like the rest of the government to prevent her and them from getting sick, and a callous disregard for the "little people" as the Representative from Kentucky described it. There were demands for her resignation and threats of impeachment. After the first few minutes, she just sat quietly. It was useless to try and defend herself. The congressmen and women were there to make points for their constituents back home, and Sybil Norcroft was the straw man for that purpose. After she was excused, and in a rare bit of bipartisanship, the members of the committee celebrated their hollow victory over the administration by introducing an obfuscation and a falsity that tarred her and shed no light on the real problems the country was facing. That evening on WWN and Wolf News, the president's approval rating was 8.5% and Sybil's 8.6%. At least she was doing better than President Willets.

White House Conference Center [an annex building of the White House], 726 Jackson Place in Washington, D.C., April 26, 2016, 0800 hrs
-Present: POTUS, VPOTUS, DCIA, JCS, Surgeon General Sybil Norcroft, CIA, DFBI, Attorney General, DATF, Speaker of the House, Senate Majority Leader, Secretaries of Defense, State, Transportation, and HHS
Re: Martial law.

The mood in the annex building was below somber. The president made no attempt at humor or ice-breaking chit-chat.

"It comes as no surprise to any of you that the level of civil unrest and criminal activity has become something beyond what we can deal with using ordinary judicial and law enforcement methods. People are no longer safe in their homes, and very few brave souls dare to venture out. This is especially true in the rural areas of the country where mobs of city dwellers are invading in the vain hope that they will be safe from the flu out there in the open spaces and fresh air. While the infection and death rates are, indeed, very high in the congested areas, the invasion of the rural areas has only spread the misery to the country people. Our prisons are overflowing; our hospitals are crowded beyond any kind of safe level; and our doctors, nurses, police officers, and courts are inundated. In short, there is a breakdown of public order here much the same as is occurring throughout the rest of the world.

"The mood of the people is one of anger, fear, and desperation. They no longer respect the law or each other. We have reached the point that the poet, Yeats described:

"Turning and turning in the widening gyre
The falcon cannot hear the falconer;
Things fall apart; the center cannot hold;
Mere anarchy is loosed upon the world,
The blood-dimmed tide is loosed, and everywhere
The ceremony of innocence is drowned;
The best lack all conviction, while the worst
Are full of passionate intensity."

"This cannot go on. We in the government cannot allow our society to come apart at the seams any longer. It is, therefore, with a heavy heart, that I am going to declare martial law throughout the United States beginning at five o'clock EST today."

Although the authorities sitting in the colonial revival building located across Pennsylvania Avenue had seen it coming and were very well aware that the same ostensibly draconian measures were now in place in the U.K., Germany, France, the Netherlands, Greece, Israel, Portugal, and South Africa, it was a sobering, even frightening, realization of how severe the pandemic really was. There was not a person in the room who doubted the necessity of the declaration, and not a person who relished even the thought of having it take place.

The weary and frightened citizens of the United States were quietly glad that the government was taking action. They feared the rioting, the shortages, and the seemingly unstoppable infectious disease that was eroding away the fiber of their society. The response of the news media, the political parties, the activists, and the general public—all of that conscious understanding aside—was stunning to President Willets and his close confidants in the administration, the Congress, and in the judiciary.

The day the announcement was made, and the National Guard from every state in the union, marched into the major cities in the country, there was a hellfire of condemnation from television reporters and pundits, Republicans and Democrats, pulpits, mosques, and synagogues. The next morning the factions of the Tea Party coalesced into a unitary angry opposition party which formulated articles of impeachment for every official in the healthcare system of the federal government and dared the senators and congressmen to defy them. As never before, an ecumenical spirit united Catholics, Protestants, Seventh Day Adventists and Mormons with all three branches of Judaism and even Sunnis and Shi'ites; and they marched in the largest protest march ever staged in the Washington Mall. The military and law-enforcement officers in charge of enforcing martial law bombarded their senior officers and the president with questions.

Finally, the president decided that—since the march appeared to be peaceful for the time being—they could march. But, he instructed the officers on the scene to make it clear that the first hint of violence would bring in the National Guard. To punctuate that statement, the Virginia and Maryland National Guard units surrounded the mall and stood fully armed at parade rest as the marchers ranted, shouted, and made speeches.

Wisconsin Avenue, NW, Georgetown, Washington D.C., April 30, 2016, 1900 hrs

Sybil and Cerisse cleared away the dinner dishes, and Charles rinsed them and put them in the dish washer. Per a family council which voted to avoid unpleasant conversation during meals, the Danielses enjoyed a short break from the violence and hatred that was swirling around them. But it was time to talk.

Charles took his prerogative as the family spokesman to sum up their situation as he saw it, "The mood of the people is so angry that they can no longer think. Ordinary friendly neighbors are terrified and becoming dangerous to anyone who crosses their paths. Look at us. We can't go out of the house with any feeling of safety. We face bandits, kidnappers, and all sorts of criminals who are taking advantage of the approaching collapse of civil society. And that is not even the biggest fear we should have. The flu is getting worse all the time.

"We are not quite at the point where ragged men pulling carts move through our neighborhoods and shout, 'bring out your dead, bring out your dead.' But we are not so far off. Morgues are storing bodies and are running out of freezer space. Mortuaries have run out of caskets. I read somewhere that casket making has become one of the most prominent businesses in the country. My dear ones, we have to do something different, and that is why I wanted us to have a formal and serious discussion tonight."

Sybil added, "I don't disagree, Charles. I have been keeping something from the two of you, and it is time for you to know the whole truth. The president, the CDC people, and my people at the Surgeon General's office as well as other government leaders have been receiving threats. People as diverse as Michigan survivalist militia people, radicalized jihadists, Tea Party extremists, and even an obscure Mormon bunch calling themselves the Danites, have issued threats— serious ones apparently—against all of us. I am waiting for a call from the president's office about a planned move to what they like to call 'an undisclosed location' where we can be surrounded by a secure protection unit. Life as we have known it has changed beyond anything I could ever have imagined."

Charles turned to Cerisse, "Your turn, kiddo. What do you see happening in your world?"

"Daddy, it is the same for me. My school is closed by order of the president. It is too dangerous for any kind of assembly of people—even schools or church gatherings. I can't get to see my friends. My application to Howard University has been put on indefinite hold. The only colleges and universities still in session are those in rural areas, and even those schools are making day-to-day decisions about keeping their doors open. This is the kind of thing I lived with in the Congo, but I never had an inkling that America...America! could get into such a state."

"I suppose I could turn tail and run. Quit my job and let someone else put on the hazmat suits and tend to the sick and dying and to endure the insults and threats from the very people we are working to protect. But it goes against everything I believe to be a quitter because the going is rough. Besides, we have to keep on fighting. The whole human race can't just lie in bed and wait for death."

"What about the impeachment proceedings? Where is that headed at the moment?"

"To reality, Charles. All of us involved in health care at the national level and every officer who is part of maintaining martial law are going to face the Law and Order committee of Congress on May the tenth. The Congress will initiate and decide on the final articles of impeachment; they will decide which of us or even all of us are to be 'impeached' by a simple majority vote and then the actual trial will be conducted in the Senate. The Senators will decide the guilt or innocence of us by a 2/3rds majority and will determine the disposition of each of the 'impeached'—the worst penalty being removal from office. Because the president is under impeachment, the Chief Justice of the Supreme Court will preside. I could be out of a job. If my many detractors want to pursue it further I maybe could even go to prison, by the end of May."

"I don't want us to split up, Sybil; but I can't keep you safe; and you will probably have to go with the government into a secure seclusion. Cerisse and I will go to California and live with the ranch people—Jose and Maria Innocenta Pomposo-Alvarez, Donita Pomposo, Pancho and Carlita Rodriguez, and Marcos and Viviana Hernandez. I called them yesterday, and they expressed their love for you and their total willingness to help us and hide us. I told them you probably would not be able to come."

"They are such lovely people. I hate to put them out. I hate the very thought that we have to do this, but we do. I think it would be a good idea for you to take the corporate jet tomorrow night and don't tell anyone else where you're going. We can always talk on our cells or text or e-mail, maybe even Skype."

They agreed on that part of their family plan. The Secret Service and the Department of State Bureau of Diplomatic Security Washington Regional Security Office handled the transfer of Sybil and her colleagues in the administration and health care leadership to Fort Meade, Maryland. The Directorate of Plans, Training, Mobilization and Security supervised their stay including the secrecy. A security specialist army unit supplemented the Secret Service and State Department Security details. It was as pleasant a confinement as could be arranged, but still confinement. Even the president chafed under the restrictions.

Chapter Fifteen

United States Senate Chamber, May 14, 2016, 1000 hrs

Martial law was well established, and a measure of calm had begun to return to the country. Cerisse Daniels's observation about the curious aspect of the pandemic that it seemed to skip teenagers was beginning to bear fruit in the DHCPP [Division of High-Consequence Pathogens and Pathology] and VSPB [Viral Special Pathogens Branch] research on the H5N1 virus and vaccine. Their genome studies had advanced to the point that they were able to find an epigenetic on-off switch set of genes which were "on" in teenagers and people who had survived illness from the virus and was "off" in the rest of the people. Furthermore, two drugs were beginning to show progress: testosterone in short high dosing schedules over three days added to acyclovir in a single massive intravenous dose, was effective in chickens to prevent, ameliorate symptoms, and even, in many cases, to eradicate the disease. The first human experimentation was in the advanced stages of planning. The HCPP and VSPB kept the rest of the world in the loop. For the first time, there was hope.

That did not alter the course of justice; the House Judiciary Committee decided there was just cause and sent the measure to the floor for consideration of drafting articles of impeachment. Congress debated for three days then voted to impeach the president and eleven other officials—an action similar to a court indictment—and on May 14, the Senate of the United States met to conduct the trial. Chief Justice August Reynolds Clarkson was present to serve as the judge; Vice-President Tanner L. Oldroyd—designated by the Constitution as, ex officio, President of the United States Senate—was present to preside; and all of the defendants—including Sybil Norcroft, the Surgeon General—were present in the Senate Chamber.

Those members of the public who had brought the original petition, the cabinet, all nine members of the Supreme Court, very carefully selected members of the House, the Department of Justice, and the press filled the gallery. The House managers were seated—as is tradition—beside the quarter-circular tables on the left side of the chamber. There was a murmuring hush in the room. Vice-President Oldroyd called for order, and the chamber fell silent.

"While the rules of the Senate permit the respondents to appear in person or be represented by counsel, all respondents are here with their attorneys and plan to give testimony. All respondents have filed answers to the articles brought against them and all have argued that the charges listed do not constitute sufficient grounds for impeachment. The House has filed a replication to the respondents' answers, and the pleadings have been completed with a rejoinder, surrejoinder, and similiter. Those proceedings are part of the record and available to all members of the Senate. A copy has been previously given to each senator and the respondents. All respondents have their attorneys here and at appropriate intervals they may be allowed to speak. I, the President of the Senate, will act in my capacity to direct or to limit the duration of questions and responses as I see fit.

"Several witnesses have been subpoenaed and are present in the chamber this morning. They will be called by the respective sides and understand that they will be subject to cross-examination. Mr. Speaker, you may proceed."

Speaker Sengupta—acting as the chairman of the committee of managers—the prosecutors—stood and recited what he and his committee of House leaders considered to be the most significant articles in the impeachment proceedings. He was brief and used his opening statement to emphasize that the president and all of the other respondents had so grossly overstepped the limits of their powers that their actions amount to having committed treason.

He concluded with an historical argument, "The fathers of the Constitution debated the wording of the impeachment clauses extensively. Early on they considered 'corrupt conduct', then 'malpractice or neglect of duty'. Still later, the wording was changed to 'treason, bribery, or corruption', and finally settled on 'treason or bribery' alone. Unsatisfied, George Mason held that "treason or bribery" was too narrow a definition and proposed adding the term 'mal-administration' but finally compromised and switched to 'other high crimes and misdemeanors' against the state'.

"The House did not hear sufficient evidence to include bribery for any of these respondents. In fact, other than in their abuse of power, they were quite selfless. However, the House did agree with those who brought complaints before it that the president did act in such an arrogant and autocratic manner as to appear to be seeking the power of a king; and that is something that this nation has never tolerated in its elected or appointed officers. It is the contention of the framers of these articles of impeachment that Parker Conrad Willets acted so intensely in that manner as to constitute treason."

He took a sip of water.

"He certainly committed 'high crimes and misdemeanors'. During the imposition of martial law, people died when law enforcement officers and military officers acted against the people under the color of authority. They are responsible for their own actions and cannot hide behind the *befehl ist befehl* [command is command] that Nazi defendants claimed in the Nuremburg trials. Let there be no mistake, the commander-in-chief bears the ultimate responsibility. Property was confiscated by eminent domain with no heed to due process. The manufacturing plants of pharmaceutical companies were temporarily taken, and the employees of those companies were forced to make vaccines under government orders. Notwithstanding the result—quick, efficient, and effective treatment for the scourge of the H_5N_1 influenza epidemic—the methods are the very antithesis of the American way. No government in this country for any reason has the authority or the right to function above the law."

His presentation took ten minutes. He was sweating from his efforts by the time he finished. His witnesses included such victims as Buy-Rite Pharmaceuticals CEO Cramer Montgomery, and the President of the Teamsters Union Mike Broadman whose union had been nationalized to keep the trucks rolling; so, the vaccines and drugs could be distributed. The president of the newly re-constituted Unified Tea Party—no longer just a movement—who vociferously decried the trampling on of the rights of good, God-fearing Americans to choose whether or not their children should be immunized. He singled out as particularly egregious the heavy-handed actions of the Surgeon General Sybil Norcroft. He emphasized that "the woman is a well-known atheist, Bible hating evolutionist, enemy of God and the good white Anglo-Saxon Protestant Americans."

The prosecution lasted a full day with almost no objections by the defense attorneys. They were content to have the witnesses be as bombastic as they wanted to be; they were their own worst enemies as they testified to the importance and relevance of their religious convictions and their knowledge that God had ordained the Constitution for freedom loving Americans whose rights were trampled by the godless power mongers. In cross-examination, all of the defense attorneys made a quiet but persistent effort to allow almost free reign to the witnesses, only taking exception to the infrequent times when the witnesses resorted to conveying facts to which the defense attorneys took exception.

During the defense case, President Willets was the picture of calm patrician dignity. He answered forthrightly and succinctly. The gist of his argument was his assertion that he and his officers and appointees were in strict obedience to the law and its spirit. His primary responsibility, and that of his officers, was to the people—to protect them and the national security, and to defend the Constitution.

When it came time for Sybil to testify, she had become calm and determined. The arguments fielded against her were absurd in her way of thinking, and she refused to be intimidated by the Bible thumpers and the anti-evidence self-seeking politicians.

"It was and is my sworn duty to protect the health and welfare of the people of the United States of America. That requires that I make firm judgments about evidence based diagnoses and what are the best treatments. I was at the time this pandemic began and am still duty bound to pursue the course decided upon unanimously by the president and his health care officers. We moved heaven and earth to find correct diagnoses—including dealing with a frequently shifting set of mutations in a rapidly evolving, yes, evolving—virus which replicates over a million times a year. Despite those difficulties, the CDC and scientists—without recourse to the Bible or the convictions of anti-science bigots—plowed ahead and discovered areas of the viral genome where the virus was vulnerable and exploited those vulnerabilities to develop a vaccine and a course of drug therapy which began to injure the power to infect, the degree of virulence, and the rapidity of replication. As a result, I can say without reservation, we are seeing the beginning of the end of this worldwide incredible epidemic—one which dwarfs Biblical and other plagues by several exponential degrees.

"I confess to the Senate that I knowingly and freely entered into an effort to use all weapons and powers at the command of the United States and its allies to fight this awful disease. I confess that I, personally, was part of enforcing martial law against the panicked citizens who were committing murder, torture, rape, and grand theft—all in the name of some misbegotten sense of freedom and the American way. We won, and they lost; and most of you here today are alive because of the courage of the president and those who obeyed his orders. No apologies, ladies and gentlemen. Two and a half million Americans and eighty-six million people world-wide are dead from this terrible disease. Had we not moved to stop it, those numbers would have been ten times higher. I made my choice to be part of the solution. The work is still ongoing. I leave it to you to determine whether you want to be part of the problem or part of the solution. Thank you for the opportunity to address the Senate."

Chapter Sixteen

Wisconsin Avenue, NW, Georgetown, Washington D.C., May 27, 2016, 1900 hrs

After the four day-long ordeal of the trial itself, and all of the presentation of evidence and argument by the managers and the counsels for the respondents was completed, the Senate as a whole met in closed session for their deliberations. They took one day to decide whether or not to convict. They then—as the law requires—met in open session with the eyes of the world upon them. The vote was taken on each article in the impeachment one at a time and then on the articles as a whole. Hundreds of cameras recorded the proceedings for the news and for history. Doug Mason—Sybil's old friend and photographer—made sure that he captured her at her best for Wolf News. Raza Patel—reporting for WWN—got his own semi-exclusive interview.

Every Senator was present for the vote that day. The final count was 28 in favor and 72 opposed to finding any of the defendants guilty on any of the articles, and the issue passed into history. In the aftermath of the impeachment trial, there was a return to something resembling sanity and peace. The pandemic subsided to less than 100 new cases a month, and the majority of them were successfully treated. Just before the impeachment trial, Sybil's and the president's approval ratings had sunk to single digit ranges. Now—two weeks later—they were 74% and 62% respectively and climbing.

After dinner, still respecting the no-business over food rule in the family, Charles asked Sybil what she was thinking now that her ordeal seemed to be over.

"I don't know what to think. I guess I'm worn out. I am debating whether or not to resign."

"You can't do that, Mama. If you do, the bad guys will win," Cerisse said shyly, "and you won't be one of the big people anymore."

"I don't know, but maybe that's a good thing, sweetie," Sybil said and looked for an answer in her husband's strong face.

"Sybil, you know this is a time of big decisions for you. I know that the president has asked you to be his next director of the CIA. What you have to decide is whether or not you can get off the porch and run with the big dogs."

-The End-

AUTHOR CARL DOUGLASS, a former neurosurgeon turned fulltime author, writes with gripping realism because in all his books he has been there and done that in some measure. He grew up in a small town where fighting was the rule, not the exception. He was determined to escape the sameness of geography, intellectual outlook, and career prospects of the majority of his contemporaries. In complete naiveté, he applied to only one well-known major university for his undergraduate work, and to everyone's surprise, he was accepted. He found himself out of his league scholastically and had to work like a Hannibal to find a way or make one to succeed in that rarefied atmosphere. His goal of success was to become a neurosurgeon, and he did it. His career in academia and the military as well as his work as a medical humanitarian provided the background to produce the riveting tales that have made their way into his remarkable books.

Sybil Norcroft Book Six

Running With The Big Dogs

The Russian mafia decides to take advantage of the deteriorating economic situation in the U.S. by staging a sophisticated raid on the New York Stock Market which nearly brings the U.S. to its knees. The president takes the extraordinary measure of accusing the president of Russia of complicity and threatens him with retaliation. The Russian cyber world crumbles around him, and the president signals his counterpart in the United States that he will rein in the Russian mafia. The cybertage being suffered in Russia comes to an abrupt halt as does the concentrated attack on the institutions of capitalism in America.

The Russian mafia retaliates by kidnapping four daughters of important American government officials—including Cerisse Daniels, the DCIA's beloved little daughter. Once again, Sybil must face the bear in his cave. She and her most trusted agents launch countermeasures fraught with personal physical danger, the danger of creating an international incident, and the very real danger of a calamitous, even fatal failure. There is no question about the fact that Sybil Norcroft is running with the big dogs.

Sybil has a revealing discussion with the president when his vice-president becomes very ill. The president observes, "You know—if you become the vice-president—you will be the first woman ever to do so, just like you became the first woman DCIA. Who knows? While you are very unlikely ever to become the First Lady, maybe you will be the first among ladies—the president of the United States. I don't think your career is over, yet, my friend."